# HIS BEST MAN

## SHIELDED HEARTS 7

### ELLE KEATON

Edited by Alicia Z. Ramos

Cover by Cate Ashwood

❀ Created with Vellum

*For my family.*
*For friends to lovers.*
*For all those authors who have gone before me and know each time is the scariest time.*
*For Alicia, I hope Rod and Travis are what you imagined they would be.*
*For all the different kinds of families.*
*Thank you,*
*Elle*

# ACKNOWLEDGMENTS

Dedication and Acknowledgements

Once again I thank my editor Alicia Z. Ramos for her dedication and hard work, for going above and beyond the call of editorial duty (even if this book was her idea in the first place) and helping His Best Man come to life. Although I will say it wasn't my idea that she head off to the wilds of Scotland!
His Best Man is dedicated to Alicia, without her it would never have happened.
Also, to my husband Erik. He knows my author cycle and knows when I get frustrated and need an ear. He knows how to listen and how to get me back from the proverbial ledge.
Thank you so much Erik, you are amazing.
To my readers, without you none of this would be true.
From the very beginning you have had faith in me, often when I didn't have any in myself. That is a priceless gift.
Thank you.
I hope you love Travis and Rod like I do.
Thank you also to, the John Deere corporation, the Kellogg corporation for Tony the Tiger, Pokémon, Steven Spielberg and

Harrison Ford for Raiders of the Lost Ark, Andrew Z. Davis for Volcano, Jan de Bont for Twister. Anyone I have failed to mention is my fault alone.

Cheers,
Elle K.

Rod fumbled with the pen he'd found nestled amongst a stash of other mostly useless writing instruments in Michael Walker's study. The myriad half-used golf pencils weren't sharpened, and most of the pens were out of ink —except, of course, the single permanent marker. Was it a rule that the only pen left that worked was always the one you wanted to use the least? And why did people keep unsharpened pencils? Especially golf pencils.

It had been equally difficult finding a piece of paper, but Rod eventually discovered a small note pad with a few pieces of lined paper left on it in a bottom drawer. He had to hurry or someone, Travis's mom with his luck, would find him in here and ask what he was doing. He heard a noise in the hallway and ducked behind the desk, his heart pounding. Feeling stupid, he peeked around the edge and watched Travis's younger sister walk by, heading toward the kitchen. When the coast was clear, he took the ridiculous pen and the pad of paper and went to hide in the downstairs bathroom.

Rod's hand trembled as he tried to think what he needed to write. What Travis would understand. He had to be clear—not that Travis was stupid, but he didn't get nuances. Rod wasn't going to declare his love for Travis when Travis had *just* announced his engagement to (literally) the girl next door. Except that was pretty much what he was doing, wasn't it? And then he'd run like the coward he was.

He shook his head at himself... again. How had he not seen it coming? He was so stupid. Travis had begged him to come for Thanksgiving; he missed Rod, blah blah blah. Rod had protested but caved. He was a sucker for Travis's pleading; he always had been. Even though he knew he shouldn't, he'd accepted the invitation, erasing all the hard work he had done putting some space between himself and Trav. He hadn't arrived until Thanksgiving morning on purpose, and now he regretted coming at all. He supposed that if Travis *had* planned on telling him about his engagement, there had been no time for it before they all sat down for the big, happy meal.

When he was satisfied with what he'd written, he tore the page from the note pad, tucked it into his back pocket, and returned the pen and paper to the study. No one had come looking for him. The happy couple and everyone else had moved to the family room to celebrate and didn't miss him. God help him if Lenore discovered him sneaking upstairs, but he did, leaving the note where Travis was sure to find it and hopefully his bitch of a mother wouldn't.

Checking up and down the hallway again and not seeing anyone, a Walker family member or otherwise, but still hearing excited voices trickling from the family room, Rod let himself out the front door—a door he was more familiar with than any other—and headed to his truck.

Instead of starting the engine, he released the parking brake and rolled out of the driveway. At the junction with the main road, he turned the key and the engine started with a reassuring rumble. Snowflakes were falling and beginning to stick on the cold pavement. He cranked up the heat and plugged in his iPod. It was going to be a long drive to Skagit.

THE FORD'S engine ticked rhythmically as it cooled after the trip, a spare, lonely sound. The storm had quieted, for the moment anyway. It wasn't comforting, though. Instead it reminded Rod he was alone. Twenty-eight, and he'd wasted a good amount of his life hoping Travis would realize how Rod felt and even return the feelings. Hope was a brutal emotion.

He rolled his neck, making a popping noise that echoed in the cab. Rod was drained, bone-tired and emotionally spent. The return drive from Walla Walla had been hellish in the early-winter storm. It had been foolish to leave when snow was falling as thick as it had been, but he couldn't have stayed another minute. He might have said or done something he would forever regret. At least this way Travis was out of his life; the cut was clean. There would be a scar, but it would heal. The miles between them would help.

The highway to Snoqualmie Pass had been littered with jackknifed semis and stalled minivans full of exhausted families trying to get home, dads outside in the snow trying to fit tire chains. The weather had turned what was normally a six-hour drive to Skagit into a six-hour drive to Ellensburg and a chilly nap at the Indian John Hill rest stop on the wrong side of the pass. By the time he woke, the pass had been closed for avalanche control. Another ten hours and here he was in Skagit, finally.

Skagit was home now.

Rod recalled his first visit to the Walker household after he came out during his freshman year of college. Lenore Walker had trapped him in the spotless white kitchen between the main course and dessert and informed him that she'd heard he was "a gay" and he should know they didn't "condone that lifestyle." Because he was Travis's friend of so many years he was allowed to continue to visit, but he understood he wouldn't be allowed to bring a guest, right? And wasn't that just fucking generous of her. Rod had never told Travis what his mother said that day. He'd also largely stopped accepting Travis's invitations to holiday dinners. But he'd never been able to stay completely away.

Why had he given in to Travis's pleading? Somebody in Skagit would have offered him a place at their table, or he could have caught whatever new action movie was opening.

He sucked in a deep breath, trying to get himself under control. The nearly twenty-four-hour trip had not calmed him down. He wanted a drink, which was why he was parked in front of his favorite bar in Skagit. Actually, he needed several drinks. He needed to drink until he couldn't see straight or think about Travis.

Rod was going to give himself one night to get utterly stinking drunk, to allow the self-pity to flow from his veins. Then he was going to buckle up and put Travis where he belonged, far away from Rod's stupid fragile heart. For real. Forever.

The truck's engine stopped ticking, and the silence in the cab was overwhelming. The cold damp of Skagit's late November snuck in through the truck's vents and slight gaps where the thirty-year-old driver's side door no longer fit the frame exactly true. He glanced at his phone. Jeez, he'd been parked in front of the Loft for forty-five minutes. The wind buffeted the truck as it picked up again, bringing freezing rain with it.

The texts and missed call from Travis he continued to ignore.

He opened the door and slid off the truck's bench seat, stiff from sitting and driving for so long. His knees buckled slightly on impact. God, he felt like an old man. Straightening and stretching, he slammed the door shut behind him, not bothering to lock it. If anyone wanted to steal a two-tone beige 1984 Ford F-150, they were welcome to it. Nobody drove a stick anymore anyway.

The Loft was much busier than Rod expected. He'd hoped to be able to hang out and mope semi-privately. This late on Black Friday—ha, it truly was a black Friday for him—folks should have been at home watching crappy movies and being with their families. Instead, the Loft was full of customers laughing and having a gay old time. Rod found the noise and laughter jarring after the silence of his truck, and the sight of male couples dancing together on the small dance floor made his heart clench painfully.

He stood just inside the doorway for a second before the bartender, his friend Cameron McCullough, noticed him. Cam sketched a quick wave, and Rod crossed the bar to sit at his usual spot. He was ready to drink his trouble away, for the night at least.

It took two stiff vodkas on an empty stomach for the whole story to come pouring out. How, without warning, Travis had announced to his entire family during Thanksgiving dinner that he and Lisa Harris were getting married. How Rod had managed to act pleased for the happy couple while his heart was shattering into a million pieces inside his body. Not just his heart; it had felt like his whole body was shattering. He had no idea how he'd managed to hold it together until he'd been able to sneak away.

Unfortunately, he hadn't been able to sneak away in time, had he? An hour or so after the meal, Rod had been in the family room fielding meaningless questions from Travis's younger sister about the past summer's firefighting and what he was doing in Skagit and trying to avoid Travis, when Travis had tracked him down. Even before Travis opened his mouth, Rod knew he didn't want to hear the question. Travis's pleading sky-blue gaze had kept Rod pinned to the spot, helpless to say no.

A carbon copy of her older brother, Abigail had watched them with big eyes, waiting breathlessly for Rod's response. Of course he'd had to say yes. Yes, he would be Travis's best man. Maybe by the time the wedding came around it wouldn't feel like he'd swallowed broken glass. Anything was possible.

Telling Cameron about it made the hurt more authentic. Rod's heart physically hurt, clenching around a jagged shard of grief that was going to make him bleed out. Funny how he'd always mocked the term "broken heart." He'd never had one before, had he? Before this weekend, he'd held out hope. The stupid thing—the most incredibly stupid thing of all—was, he'd known it was coming. Lenore was always asking when Travis was going to "settle down," and Rod had known that when push came to shove, Travis would never pick him.

"Another double, hold the ice."

Cameron generously offered to take Rod home to his cabin, driving Rod's beat-up truck himself instead of forcing Rod to be alone. Rod was childishly (and drunkenly) happy about the decision; being alone was not something he wanted tonight. Plus he might crack and answer Travis's texts. He needed to distance himself a little before he answered, otherwise he might say something he would regret. Rod finished his drink; before he could ask, another appeared in its place.

It was funny; after worrying for so long about telling Travis how he felt about him—too scared to risk their friendship—now Rod was going to be the one to put a hold on it. He didn't think he could maintain the level of closeness they'd been oper-ating at for most of their lives. They'd been best friends since the third grade. They'd gone to high school and then college together. Travis joined a fraternity, the same one his dad had been in, while Rod lived in the dorms. Later, they'd roomed together in off-campus housing. Travis had been there when Rod's family imploded; he'd taken him to their favorite bar and gotten him drunk enough to forget about it for a little while.

After graduation they'd decided to join the Forest Service as seasonal firefighters. Rod had wanted to pay off the remainder of his student loans and had no idea what to do with his English degree. Travis? Well, he'd always been at Rod's side, so it hadn't seemed odd that he decided to join up too. Rod was used to having Travis by his side, at his back—in his life.

Travis's folks hadn't been happy about the firefighting; it took Travis away from the family farm during the summer and early fall when he'd otherwise have gone back to help out. Lenore and Michael acted like the time away was a vacation. Rod wondered if they realized how close to death their son had come fighting fires; how many times Travis had saved Rod's ass and vice versa. And even if they did both enjoy the work, surely Travis deserved to have some fun?

If Travis was getting married, he would be taking over the Walker empire. He would be home every night safe and sound. So that was another part of his life Rod needed to say goodbye to. Rod had thought Travis was dreading when it would be time for him to take over the business. Maybe he'd been the one in denial, not Trav? Rod had hoped so hard that Travis would find a way out. Instead he was further entrenched than before. Rod knocked his drink back, letting the sounds of laughter and music mute his unpleasant thoughts.

SOFT SCRAPING SOUNDS Rod didn't immediately recognize intruded into his slowly awakening consciousness. It was oddly quiet; there were no street sounds, cars starting or doors slamming shut. The huff of wind rustling through trees and rubbing branches against windows was at the forefront, followed by the creaking sound of someone trying to move quietly. His eyes flew open. The ceiling above him was unfamiliar.

He shut his eyes again. The night before came rushing back. He'd been at the Loft, and now he was at Cameron's, and he'd gotten up in the night and been thoroughly sick. He tried to stifle his groan of embarrassment and agony from his hangover. Cam, or maybe Ira, chuckled, the sound drifting from the loft above.

Waking up at Ira and Cam's cabin turned out to *almost* be more uncomfortable than nearly breaking down when Travis announced his engagement. He recognized his intense jealousy where Ira and Cam were concerned, a feeling he didn't like. As soon as he could, he took his leave, thanking the two men profusely but needing to be alone.

He lingered on the porch of the cabin for a minute, breathing the cool air deep into his lungs and trying to shake the stupid hangover headache. The day was crisp and clear; there was only a light breeze now, the tree branches overhead were hardly moving, and the November sunlight was painfully bright. Yesterday's storm had blown itself out, leaving only a few downed branches as evidence. The last leaf stragglers were gone from the maples and cottonwood, leaving the trunks bare and exposed to the elements. Very much how Rod's soul felt.

# 2

The hell, where was Rod? Travis scoured the house, even going down the basement stairs, although what Rod would be doing down there was beyond Travis. The basement was full of years' worth of junk. Rod was not hiding in the appliance graveyard or hanging out with the power tools.

Travis lived at the family home when he was in Walla Walla. He'd prefer his own place, but whenever he brought it up, both his parents would point out how practical it was for him to stay home, and his mom would start to tear up. Travis figured the fight wasn't worth it, and anyway, sometimes he spent four or five months away during fire season, so an apartment would be sitting empty.

Being away from Walla Walla every summer was emotionally steep but worth the price. When he was home he was reminded at every turn that it was his duty to take over the farm, that the property had been in the family for four generations, that he was the last Walker boy... this was usually followed by lamentations that Travis wasn't married, there were no grandchildren, and his mother worried about his future. Travis couldn't help but think it seemed like his mother was a lot more worried about his "legacy" than he was.

Travis hated the weight of generational responsibility for the Walker farm. Some days he could actually feel it pressing down on him. Gravitational force was a constant, but it seemed like it doubled when he thought about being stuck in Walla Walla forever.

It was expected that he would take on the farm, be a wheat farmer for the rest of his life, and Travis hated it. He hated even more that he was good at ag science. His parents had insisted on his major. He'd liked most of his classes fine, just not when the knowledge meant that he was going to live out his life in a small, dusty corner of southeast Washington. Rod was the only one who truly understood how he felt.

Where *was* he, anyway? Rod usually hung out in the TV room whenever he was over. The TV room was their comfort zone; had been since they started college. It was game time, the parents were in the living room now, and Travis could finally relax. His folks had finally said goodbye to Lisa and her dad. Lisa'd acted like she wanted to stay, but Travis had made it clear he and Rod were gonna to play some *Call of Duty*. His best buddy had made the long trip here, and Travis wanted to hang out and relax.

This was Travis's favorite part of the four-day holiday weekend, other than the food. This was what he lived for: staying up late playing games with Rod and shooting the breeze, remembering all the stupid stuff they'd done. The past couple of months had been weird, with Travis at home in Walla Walla and Rod three hundred miles away in Skagit.

Plus, Travis's palms were still clammy from making the engagement announcement during dinner, and he needed to work off some nervous energy shooting stuff. He hadn't exactly planned to tell everyone during dinner, but there hadn't seemed like a better time to get it over with. His mother had actually shrieked with joy. He shook his head as he made his way back upstairs to the kitchen.

His sister had the refrigerator door propped open against her hip, hunting for a snack. Wasn't it funny how you could eat until you thought you were going to pop and somehow manage to be hungry only a few hours later? Strangers often thought he and Abs were twins; Abigail was almost as tall as Travis, and they had the same color hair and eyes. Travis was older, but Abigail constantly reminded him *she* was more mature.

"Abigail, where's Rod? Have you seen him? I can't find him anywhere."

Abigail cocked her head over her shoulder to look over at him with an expression Travis couldn't quite translate. He wasn't always good at reading people. He needed them to tell him what they were thinking.

"He left. I saw his truck pull out of the driveway." She pulled a plate of turkey out of the fridge and started to make herself a sandwich.

Travis was speechless for a minute. Rod had left? Where would he go? *Why* would he go?

"He left? When? The roads are going to be terrible! Why would he leave without saying goodbye?" There'd been warnings all week about a winter storm on its way that was going to bring snow east of the Cascades and rain and wind to the west side of the state.

"Gee, Trav, I don't know, maybe because you forgot to mention to him that you were getting engaged?" Abigail let out a derisive scoff. "And to Lisa Harris, of all people." She dumped a spoonful of cranberry sauce on the turkey before laying the second piece of bread across the meat.

"Don't hold back, Abigail, tell me how you really feel. What's wrong with Lisa? She's nice, and we've known her forever."

"Lisa's been obsessing over you forever. She used to try and pump me for information about you: what did you like, *who* did you like... I just have a bad feeling." She shrugged. "If I'm wrong, I'll buy you a beer. Anyway, don't you think 'what's wrong' is a question you should have asked *before* you asked her to marry you?" She took a big bite of her sandwich, chewing and swallowing while she waited for his answer.

"Jeez, Abs." She glowered at the use of her childhood nickname; "Abs" did not make her happy. "Like I said, I've known her forever. She's always been nice to me, and Mom and Dad— well, Mom seems to like her." His mom was the only one who mattered; their dad tended to stay quiet during family discussions. "Besides, I didn't really ask her. We kind of agreed together."

"You are so stupid. God. How did you survive to adulthood? You know how? I'll tell you how: Rod saved your ass time after time. You wouldn't be alive if it wasn't for him. I mean, seriously, if you are going to use the excuse; I'm sorry, 'reason'"—she actually made air quotes—"that you asked Lisa to marry you because you've known her forever, why didn't you ask Rod? You've known him longer."

She muttered something else under her breath as she stomped away, plate in hand, but Travis didn't hear what she said. He couldn't hear anything past "ask Rod"; there was a weird roaring in his ears. Travis trailed after his sister as she marched out of the kitchen and up the back stairs toward their bedrooms.

Abigail's room was at the top of the stairs and looked much as it had throughout their childhood. The walls were a light pink, matching the comforter on her bed, and several throw pillows covered in a darker pink fabric were propped on top of the bed. It looked pretty, Travis supposed, and the white carpet made the colors pop. Their mom had designed everything from a catalog picture she'd seen.

"I can't ask Rod to marry me." Why were they even talking about this?

Putting her plate down on the pretty bedside table, Abigail threw herself on the bed and began shoving the pillows to the floor. "I hate these pillows, I hate these colors, I hate all of it. I don't know why Lenore insists on decorating my room; I'm never moving back for good. And yes you can, same-sex marriage has been legal in Washington since 2012."

"I mean..." Travis's voice trailed off. Why was the idea of marrying Rod throwing him off?

Abigail finished ravaging her bed, going so far as to turn the comforter over to show a pale mint green on the other side. She flopped back on the mattress and narrowed her eyes at him. The room was quiet while Travis waited for her to say something else. She had more on her mind, he was certain of that.

Travis leaned back against the doorframe, feigning calmness.

Finally she broke the silence. "Travis, you *are* gay, aren't you?"

"Shhh! Jesus, you don't want Mom hearing you tossing around words like that, she'll lecture you for hours." They weren't an uber-religious family, but Walla Walla was a conservative small town, and Lenore placed herself firmly in the "gays are bad" camp.

Abigail rolled her eyes. "You know what? She's not the boss of me anymore. I'm an adult. Are. You. Gay. Travis."

He opened his mouth to deny his sexuality, but something in Abigail's expression and stormy blue eyes made him stop. When the subject came up—and it never had with his little sister, thank you very much—Travis said he was bi. He did *think* he was bi. He'd had sex with women and enjoyed it enough, but in reality was he wasn't attracted to a lot of women. He tended toward an athletic and tomboyish physical type. Tiny feminine women did nothing for him.

"Bi, mostly."

"Bi," she repeated, raising both eyebrows.

"I've had sex with women." Travis scuffed a toe along the pristine carpet, thinking about how he spent the off time during fire season. If he wasn't hanging out with Rod, he was horizontal with whoever made themselves available. Mostly of the male variety.

"Having sex with women doesn't make you straight, Trav, or bi for that matter."

He knew that.

"Why are we discussing my, uh, bi-ness when I just got engaged to Lisa?"

His sister rolled her eyes up to the ceiling again. At this rate they were going to freeze that way.

"Okay, big brother, you are bi. You're right, I'm not inside your head. I apologize."

Abigail started to say something else, but Travis heard footsteps on the stairs behind him, followed by their mother's voice.

"Sweetlings," she called out. Travis and Abigail both cringed. Abigail jumped up, grabbing the pillows off the floor where she'd flung them, and quickly began rearranging her bed. Travis turned around to greet Lenore, buying Abs some time.

"Mom." Travis tried to summon a real smile for her, but it felt contrived and uncomfortable. The conversation with Abigail had him off balance.

"It's so nice to see the two of you getting along. I'm sure Abby is just as excited as I am that Lisa is joining the family. Oh, Travis," Lenore clasped her hands, "you've made me so happy! I was getting worried you'd never settle down and give me grandbabies."

Abigail appeared beside Travis. "Mom, you can't go imagining grandkids, they're not even married yet. What if it doesn't work out?" Bless Abs for putting it out there, but no way was Lenore going to entertain the idea of Travis and Lisa not working out when the engagement had been public knowledge for less than twenty-four hours.

Frankly, Travis hadn't put much thought into the engagement at all... and he was beginning to realize this was a serious problem. He'd been out drinking at the Green Lantern with Lisa and a few other old friends. When the others had left, he and Lisa stayed to finish their drinks and have a few more. Travis liked Lisa's company enough, they'd got to talking about life, marriage (the details were murky there), and the next thing Travis knew, they'd decided it would be perfect if they got married.

They celebrated by going to Lisa's place and having drunken sex. At least, Travis had woken up in her bed naked with the covers all over the place, so he figured they'd had sex. He'd let out a breath he hadn't known he was holding when he saw the used condom in the trash next to the bed.

"When are we going to tell our families?" Lisa was awake now, watching as Travis pulled on his clothes from the night before, her long dark hair splayed across a pillow.

"Thanksgiving dinner?" Doing it then would be easiest. Everybody would be there; he'd do it quick, so it would be over with—like pulling off a Band-Aid.

Travis cringed at the memory.

Lenore kept talking as if Abigail hadn't spoken at all. "I was thinking, a spring wedding will be perfect. After all, there is no reason to wait. Tomorrow I'm going to call and see if the Grange is available in May or June. Your dad and I got married in June."

"Mom, I'll probably be called for fire season in May," Travis said, trying to slow her down.

Lenore stared at Travis for a second, her mouth slightly open, before replying, "Travis, the time for that kind of thing is over. You're a family man now. Tomorrow at breakfast we'll talk dates and, as I said, I'll call around. If the Grange is taken, maybe the gazebo at the park. Don't sleep in too late; we have so much to talk about. Abigail, don't leave that plate up here." With that she turned to make her way down the short hallway and back downstairs.

The two of them were quiet for a moment, staring at each other, and then Abigail spoke. "Wow, it's even worse than I thought. I'm going to bed, brother. Good luck in the morning." She shut the door behind her, leaving Travis standing in the hallway wondering what the hell he had done to his life.

TRAVIS'S BEDROOM was at the far end of the hall and much larger than Abigail's; it extended the full length of the house. Six windows took up the long wall looking down into the front yard. Half the room was set up like a living room, with a TV, gaming system, and small couch to lounge on while playing or watching movies. The other half harbored a display case that held all the meaningless trophies from the various team sports he'd played throughout his school years. They were embarrassing; he didn't even want Rod seeing those stupid things. His bed, across from the TV, was queen-size, not that anyone but him would ever be sleeping in it.

Except... goose bumps spread across his skin, and Travis twitched. He'd be sleeping with Lisa, wouldn't he? And now his mom was already talking about grandkids. Travis liked kids enough, but he'd never imagined himself with a bunch of mini-me's running around.

Rod loved kids; he was a magnet for them. Rod was a magnet for all living things. Travis couldn't count how many times wounded or stray animals that animal control couldn't capture would just come right up to his best friend.

Shit. Rod. Shit, shit, shit, why had he left? Travis needed his buddy here so he could figure out why he was feeling weird and out of sorts. Rod was always patient with Travis, never making him feel stupid when he took things literally. They'd laughed over the years that they shared a brain, because there were a lot of times when one of them would say something and the other would have been thinking it. Or Travis would have an idea and Rod would know it was bad without hearing what it was. Although sometimes it was Rod with the wild idea. Travis chuckled, remembering the time they'd caught birds for Rod's animal hospital, only to have his mother scream and make them set the birds free.

He stared at his gaming system. He couldn't bring himself to load up *Call of Duty* now; he didn't feel like playing alone. He stripped down to his boxer briefs and slid under the covers where he could hide from reality. The sheets were cool and felt good against his skin. Unfortunately, this was yet another sheet-and-comforter set provided by his mother. It looked like she'd gotten ahold of a Pottery Barn catalog and gone wild. The duvet was a hideous dark green and beige covered with cowboy hats and boots surrounded by lassos, butt-ugly. Nothing Travis would pick out for himself. Well, he wouldn't be able to see it in the dark.

It was midnight, but he shot another text off to Rod anyway. Hopefully they could get together in the morning and hash whatever this was out. Travis waited a few minutes for a reply, but it had been a long day. Turning off the bedside lamp, he pulled the comforter across his body, then lay wide awake for hours, unpleasant thoughts keeping his brain from turning off.

·  ·  ·

FRIDAY MORNING CAME FAR TOO SOON. The last time he'd looked at the clock, it had been 3:48 a.m. He checked his phone first thing, but there was still no reply from Rod. He wondered where Rod had stayed the night. Now that his parents were gone from town, Rod usually slept in the Walkers' family room. Travis's mom frowned on adult sleepovers… whatever that meant. Maybe he'd had a room at one of the chain hotels in town and forgot to tell Travis. He texted again. No answer.

Breakfast was a nightmare.

When Lenore said they would talk in the morning, she had neglected to mention that Lisa and her dad would be joining them. Hadn't they all seen each other the day before? Why did they need to get together twelve hours later? Travis wanted nothing more than to sip his black coffee and try to figure out where he'd gone wrong.

He sat at the table feeling like he was being flattened by a steamroller, Wile E. Coyote–style, while his mother and Lisa discussed the upcoming wedding, making lists and searching the internet for various "must-haves." Abigail shot him sympathetic glances, but they only made Travis feel worse and more trapped and stupid, although he still hadn't entirely figured out that angle of his stupidity. Yet. He might be slow, but he always made it to the finish line.

His dad came to his rescue.

"Son, I need some help out in the small barn today. You think you can let the ladies talk wedding shop while we patch a few holes in the roof?" The "small barn" was two thousand square feet and a single story, compared to the "big barn," which was over three thousand square feet and two-and-a-half stories tall. The small barn was also out on the original Walker property east of town, so he and his dad would be gone a good portion of the day, given that the roads were icy as fuck.

"Sure, Dad."

His mom may have wanted him to stay, but she deferred to Michael when it came to the farm. Twenty minutes later they were gone from the house, heading east toward Waitsburg. Travis sent one more text to Rod. He could tell they'd been read, but the bastard hadn't bothered to respond. For the rest of the day he and his dad would be out of cell phone range. A blessing and a curse. He'd talk to Rod tonight.

## 3

Was there a word for feeling worse than utter and complete crap? Rod wasn't sure. Aside from his terrible hangover, he'd ignored Travis's texts from Thanksgiving evening and the day after. Now he felt guilty, hurt, *and* had a hangover.

The texts sat on his phone unanswered, taunting him. He shouldn't have left town like that, he knew, but he hadn't been able to stomach being around the happy couple. And he was still afraid he would say something he couldn't take back. As hurt and angry at himself as he was, Rod didn't want to cut ties with Travis. He just needed space to redefine their relationship, and for that he needed a little time and distance.

He needed a plan.

The Ford rumbled along the two-lane road as Rod drove back into Skagit from Cam's cabin. His cell phone was stuffed in the glove compartment so he wouldn't be tempted to read, or answer, any texts that might have arrived since he last looked. No, he would quietly obsess about Travis instead... as he had been since they were both sixteen.

. . .

OVERNIGHT, Travis had gone from being Rod's best friend and partner in boyhood crimes to being the half-grown man starring in Rod's budding sexual fantasies. The fantasies had evolved since then, but back then all he'd needed to do was think about Travis, about his laughing blue eyes, his stupid hair that turned almost white in the summer sun, his butt.

Rod imprinted on Travis like a duckling... except there were zero childlike feelings on Rod's part. One day they were best friends; the next, Rod was having to wear loose jeans to hide the nearly constant semi he had around his friend. Realizing he was gay but living in a conservative farming town had meant it was imperative for Rod to keep his sexuality hidden. He'd been under no illusion that there weren't people in town who would be happy to dump his body in the Walla Walla River or thrash him behind the quick-stop on the highway out of town.

He'd been lucky: as Travis's best friend, Rod was largely ignored by the set of people who spent their days making other people's lives miserable. Travis was popular and generally well-liked by everyone, and Rod swam along in his wake, accepted by the cool kids through osmosis. And Rod was still so deep in the friend zone Travis had asked him to be his best man.

Travis confessed to Rod he was bi after Rod came out to him in college, but he never acted like anything more than a friend to Rod—even though they spent almost all their time together. Pretty much the only thing they didn't do was have sex. And Travis never slept with guys when they were home. Walla Walla was women-only. Until Lisa, Rod hadn't been certain there were any home-town girls left for Travis to date, much less ask to marry him.

"Ugh," Rod groaned. The wedding was going to be a nightmare.

In college Rod had dated a couple guys and learned he mostly liked to be on the receiving end of sex, but none of them were Travis. He didn't feel a light turn on inside himself after not seeing them for a few days like he did when Travis came back from working out at the "property" for a few days. Rod had never told anyone but Cam about his feelings for Travis, but somehow his boyfriends guessed and eventually left, because who wanted to play second fiddle to the impossible?

"You spend more time with Travis than you do me," Ben had complained. "If you like him so much, why don't you date *him*?"

Well.

"Oh, look." Rod looked over his shoulder in the direction Jonah was staring. "It's your other boyfriend, Travis. I think I'll be going."

And so on, until Rod quit dating and started only hooking up with guys for sex. Then even that got depressing. When he moved to Skagit, he'd bought a dildo and a vibrator from the cleverly named "Otto's Erotica." Now that he thought back on it, safe in the warm cab of his truck, he was pathetic. Twelve years of waiting for a guy to figure out Rod was the man for him? Rod had been acting the fool, and he was done.

He was officially turning over a new leaf, starting a new life, whatever the right phrase was. Pining for Travis was over. If Rod wanted to salvage their friendship—which he did; he couldn't imagine his life without Travis in it—he needed to get over him.

Travis was going to marry Lisa Harris, and Rod would be his best man, like a best friend should.

A Steller's jay fluttered down from a cedar tree off to the right, its blue-black wings flashing in the bright sunlight. Lots of folks didn't like the jays, but Rod did; they were funny, opportunistic little birds and usually the only ones who stood up to the native corvids. Crows could bully an eagle, but Steller's jays gave them the finger.

.  .  .

THE APARTMENT WAS cold after Rod being gone for a few days. There was nothing to eat in the fridge, not that he ever kept much in it anyway. It wasn't a great apartment, but it had been what Rod could find when he'd decided to move to Skagit after fire season. The 1980s construction had never been updated... which, really, that said enough, didn't it? There was no lobby; all the units opened to the outside with a little porch area. Rod's was on the second floor, with two small flights of stairs to reach the front door.

He hadn't taken much time to furnish it; he didn't have that much stuff. At this point he had a mattress and box spring sitting on the floor of the bedroom and a tired beige couch he'd bought off a guy moving out of the unit next to him. The local thrift store had provided a decent set of dishes and a few pots and pans. Rod didn't really cook, so the pots and pans were mostly to make it look like he *thought* about cooking. Of course there was a TV for video games and movies, perched in a weird built-in entertainment center. Or at least it had come with the apartment; probably the thing was so heavy it was more trouble than it was worth to move it.

Today, after he unlocked the door and let himself inside, the starkness of the apartment hit him hard. He dropped his overnight bag in the bedroom and made himself a cup of coffee. Since he wasn't allowing himself to dwell on the state of his life, Rod spent the next hour unpacking the boxes he'd left sitting in the corner of the living room.

It was like pouring vinegar on an open wound. Every time he dipped his hand in a box, out came something associated with Travis. The baseball glove from the single year Trav convinced Rod to play. The team picture from that same year, Trav smiling and blond in the back row, Rod kneeling in the front row but off to the side, next to that jerk Brent David, who tried to trap Rod in the showers and grab his ass.

There were the sets of *Star Wars* and *Star Trek* DVDs they'd pooled their money for in college. Rod wasn't sure how they'd ended up in his collection. The two of them had argued for years about which of the two was better. Rod was firmly in Patrick Stewart's camp, while Travis harbored a ridiculous affection for the rebel outpost shenanigans. Rod shrugged and tossed the cases onto the entertainment center. And so it went.

When the boxes were empty, Rod broke them down and stacked them by the front door. Then he plopped down on the couch with his laptop and clicked open a browser. It was now or never. He clicked on the icon for a dating site. There had to be someone halfway decent living in the region.

THE MONDAY MORNING AFTER THANKSGIVING, Rod was back at work. He mostly loved his job as a school bus driver, but Mondays were always Mondays. The bus jerked to a halt, Rod pressing harder on the brake than he'd intended, but he'd only just hit the gas when he spied Jasper Ransom trotting around the corner a block away.

Technically he wasn't supposed to wait for kids more than a few minutes, but Jasper was chronically late, and Rod worried because there didn't seem to be an adult associated with him anywhere. A lot of the kids walked home on their own, but usually there was a parent or guardian on the first day of school at least. Jasper had always showed up alone.

That first week or so of driving, Jasper had been the bane of Rod's nascent career as a bus driver: not staying in his seat, yelling at the top of his lungs, running back to look out the emergency door to see and wave at whoever was driving behind them. Once Rod hit on the idea of Storyvilletime, Jasper had quieted down, and now it was often Jasper telling the other kids to calm down "cause otherwise we won't be able to write our story."

The doors folded open, and a panting Jasper climbed aboard.

"Morning, Jasper. That was pretty close, buddy."

"Morning, Mr. Beton." Jasper slid into the seat behind Rod. Rod noticed he didn't have a backpack today and was only wearing a sweatshirt and jeans despite the cold weather that had rolled into Skagit. "What are the lizards doing now?"

It was a twenty-minute ride to the school after picking Jasper and one other kid up. Frog and his friend Toad discovered a group of bad-guy lizards lurking outside the rebel compound. They were planning on tricking the lizards into a trap, but Toad suddenly needed a nap, and all the kids knew that unless Toad got his nap, something bad would happen. The school bus rolled into its spot in the school parking lot, and the kids all grumbled about having to wait to find out what happened next. Rod grinned as he said goodbye to his riders until three thirty. They were going to go nuts when Phabian Frog and Todd Toad found the hidden stash of jalapeño peppers. *Everyone* knew lizards loved hot peppers.

Rod chuckled as he pointed the school bus in the direction of the bus lot. It was nice to be back in his routine. He wondered what Travis was up to and then stopped because he couldn't go there. Wouldn't.

# 4

Travis was hiding out in his bedroom. It was the only place in the house he felt safe from his mother. He had the TV on, but he wasn't paying attention; the light from the screen flickered as the actors and stunt performers ran around jumping on each other, causing weird shadows on his bedroom walls. He wished Abigail were around, but she was back in Boise gearing up for the end of her master's degree. He flopped over onto his back to stare at the ceiling. He didn't even feel like playing a video game. Instead, he watched the shadows flick back and forth.

When was the last time he and Rod had gone this long without seeing each other? Travis didn't think there'd been one. He hated that Rod had decided to move to Skagit. They'd talked briefly on the phone a few times since Thanksgiving, but Rod seemed distracted, their conversations short, with no banter or joking around. Admittedly, Travis himself had been busy helping his dad and the Walker Enterprises permanent staff with the winter wheat. They'd planted a bit late, and the coverage wasn't what they'd been hoping for. Wind erosion was always a worry, and this year they'd already had heavy storms.

He hadn't gotten up the nerve to tell Rod what Abigail had said about marrying Rod instead of Lisa. It didn't feel like something he could pass off as a joke. It felt serious, like a heart attack. It wasn't something you just said. When Rod hadn't come for Christmas, instead telling Travis he had plans with some people he'd met in Skagit, Travis knew something was up. And how he was going to fix it when he was supposed to be marrying Lisa?

He was so fucking fucked.

Say Abigail was right and Travis was as thick as a post, completely missing that Rod... Travis couldn't think the thought. If Rod had *feelings* for Travis and Travis had been a bone brain and announced that he and Lisa were getting married... then Travis had really hurt Rod. He didn't mean to hurt Rod. If he could live his life without ever hurting Rod, that would be a good thing.

But Travis didn't know where to start to fix what had gone wrong, and now Rod was... not exactly ghosting him, but definitely keeping him at arm's length. All Travis could see in his future was a train wreck of hurt. Lisa, his mom, Rod. There was a goddamned ripple effect happening that Travis really hadn't seen coming.

Since Thanksgiving, wedding talk had overtaken nearly every conversation in the household. His mom spoke of nothing else when they were sitting around the dining room table, or in the TV room, or getting their first cup of coffee in the morning. Travis was sick of it. He listened enough to nod when he needed to, but the details were fuzzy and he didn't focus on them.

He did know Lenore hadn't been able to reserve the Grange or the gazebo. Now she was on a mission to reserve some historic barn between Waitsburg and Walla Walla. The wedding was her new hobby, and it was slowly killing him. Even Lisa seemed overwhelmed by Lenore's intensity.

A twinge of unworthy jealousy sparked because Lisa was going to get away from all this nonsense soon. Travis stomped it out. The only reason Lisa and her dad were planning a dream around-the-world trip was that Lisa's mother had insisted upon it on her deathbed only a year before. In the flickering dark of his bedroom, he admitted to himself that running away from it all sounded pretty good. But he wasn't that kind of person.

It didn't help that Rod was on the other side of the state. Normally he would be the one Travis would talk to about this sort of thing, and they would share a good laugh about how controlling Lenore was. And no, he wasn't so dense that he didn't recognize the irony there and the essence of what Abigail had said the night he announced their engagement: he was much closer to Rod than the woman he was engaged to. Or he had been.

Travis wasn't stupid; in fact, he'd graduated top of his class. He just wasn't people smart. But people liked him, and that seemed to make up for a lot of shortfalls.

THE NEXT NIGHT Lisa was over for dinner again. She and Lenore were talking about favors. Favors? Travis escorted her home afterward, walking her up the porch steps of the mother-in-law unit she lived in. After her mother had died, Lisa had moved back from the Tri-Cities to be closer to her dad. It was cold, and the scent of snow was in the air. Travis wondered, did Lisa dream of leaving Walla Walla again, of maybe having a life that wasn't horses and wheat; hot, oppressive summers and cold, foggy winters?

At the top of the steps, he gave her as quick a kiss goodbye as he could justify. In the past weeks he'd come up with every possible excuse not to be intimate with her, even though she made it painfully clear she wanted more. He'd faked a cold for a few days—before actually getting one, which was probably what he deserved. He knew he was being deceitful, dragging this out much longer than it should have gone, but he didn't know what to do. He was trapped, and he'd done it to himself. It wasn't only about Lisa. It was his mom, his dad—all the people in town who knew just one small part of him and expected his life to play out in a certain way.

Lisa's lips were nice and soft, but they did little for him. He had the traitorous thought that he hoped he wouldn't have to get drunk every time they had sex. There was going to be sex happening again at some point, but his mind kept swerving past that fact, avoiding it like a massive pothole. How much guilt was he going to have to feel before he was overwhelmed with it? Travis supposed he would find out.

"Your mom is so excited about the wedding."

All thoughts of sex with Lisa, positive or otherwise, fled. His mother tended to have that effect on him.

"I'm not complaining—it's really nice, and my dad is glad she seems to want to do everything," she hastened to explain, reaching out to hold his hand. It took everything Travis had in him to let her take it.

Travis pulled a face. "Yeah, I'm feeling pretty overwhelmed. It's been what, a month? And all she talks about is the wedding." The night before, he'd excused himself from the table and his mom had actually followed him down the hallway to the bathroom still talking about flowers and "tool" and what kind of food she wanted. He'd had to go look up tool and weddings on the internet. It took him a few minutes to figure out the right spelling. Why would he care about tulle?

"Lisa—"

"Travis—"

They both laughed nervously, the sound echoing across the front porch.

"You go first," Travis said. He needed to find a way to tell her that he had no idea what he was doing, that he needed to call it off for now. Probably forever.

Lisa looked him in the eyes, making Travis feel squirmy.

"I'm off the pill."

"Excuse me?"

"I'm off birth control. By the time dad and I get back from our trip, my body will be ready for babies."

Apparently you could know someone for years and really not know them at all.

"Babies?" Travis squeaked out.

"Our kids will be so beautiful. I can hardly wait to get pregnant."

Fucking hell.

"Lisa. I thought this was to make our parents happy, to get them off our backs about marriage. I'm not ready for kids, I don't know if I even want kids. Lisa, I can't marry you." The words just popped out. It wasn't as if Travis hadn't been thinking them almost every minute of every day, but now they'd escaped from his mouth. The look on Lisa's face would have been priceless if anything about the situation were funny.

She dropped his hand and gaped at him, her mouth hanging open as she processed what Travis had just said. Travis stuck his hands in his coat pockets, waiting for a blow of some kind. He certainly deserved it.

"You what?" Her voice rose.

"I can't marry you." He'd said it once; he'd keep saying it until she understood.

"I'm leaving on our trip in a week, and now you tell me?" Lisa's voice rose until by the end of the sentence she was screaming. The porch light next door—her dad's house—flicked on.

"I'm sorry." He was sorry; he was sorry this had ever happened and sorrier now that he couldn't go through with it.

But he couldn't. "Maybe it's good you're going away. By the time you get back, this whole thing will have blown over."

"You mean by the time I get back you will have told the whole town about me, made this my fault." Tears were streaming down her face, and Travis didn't know what to do.

"Why would I do that? This is about me, not you."

"That's what they all say, then they turn around and find another girl. I hate you, Travis. Get out of my face. I never want to see you again."

She shoved him hard. He wasn't expecting it and stumbled down the two steps to the yard below.

"Get away from me, you pig."

She fumbled in her coat pocket until she pulled out a little canister and pointed it at him. Travis had thought she was looking for her house keys. He slipped on the frosty front lawn as he ran toward his house, the frozen grass crunching under his shoes. He heard the hiss of what was probably pepper spray from behind him, but he wasn't stopping to make sure. He wobbled and nearly slipped again, scrambling around the corner before he righted himself and kept moving quickly down the sidewalk, Lisa's final "You fucking asshole!" burning his ears.

File under: things that did not go as planned. He supposed it might have gone better if he had, in fact, planned what he was going to say instead of just letting it fall from his lips. At least she was going to be gone for over a month, traveling with her dad.

Even with the specter of his mother's disappointment looming, when Travis unlocked the front door and slipped inside, he felt for the first time in weeks that maybe there was some kind of hope. If he only he could get ahold of Rod.

IN THE DAYS THAT FOLLOWED, Travis was kept busy with farm business and didn't see the harm in waiting to tell his mother the wedding was off. She was going to be mad no matter when he told her. He fully expected that Lisa would call his mom before she left, but the phone had stayed quiet, and as far as he knew, Lisa and Lenore didn't exchange emails.

Travis felt like a jackass for letting Lisa down—for getting the two of them into the situation in the first place and for the way he'd ended it. He'd hurt someone—not with intent, but he'd still hurt her. That stuff about babies freaked him out, though. Where had that come from? He gave her a few days to calm down before he tried to apologize again. It seemed wrong to let her leave without talking with her again, being honest.

The night before Lisa and her dad were due to leave, Travis tapped on Lisa's front door and waited for her to answer, shifting his weight back and forth from one foot to the other. He knew she was home; her car was parked in the driveway. There was a shuffle and a click, then Lisa opened the door a crack. From what he could see of her, she looked tired but not distraught.

"What do you want?" Not distraught; still angry.

"Can I come in for a minute? I, um, I'd like to talk to you."

She stood there for a second, obviously debating the question. Finally she opened the door wide enough for him to slip inside. She led him into the living room but didn't offer him a place to sit, instead standing with her arms wrapped protectively around herself.

"First of all, I'm sorry. I know the words probably mean nothing, but I really did not intend on hurting you."

She stared at him, eyebrows raised.

Travis took a deep breath, willing himself to do something right for once.

"I'm bi, bisexual." His voice shook a little, but he kept forcing the words out. "I've never told anyone here at home. Well, except Rod, of course. Um, anyway, I've—god, this is so stupid."

"Travis, sit down. The way you're breathing, I'm afraid you're going to hyperventilate."

Lisa waved him over to where a short countertop separated the eating area from the kitchen. There were two barstools tucked under the counter. Travis pulled one out and sat down while Lisa leaned on the other side, waiting for him to finish.

"You're bisexual, so what?"

Travis picked up a coaster that was sitting on the counter and spun it between his fingers while he talked. "I'm not ashamed of being bi, not really, except here. And because I know my parents—Lenore, at least—won't understand, I've never told them."

"It's Rod, isn't it?" Lisa saved him from his rambling. "I should have realized sooner."

Travis stared at her for a second. "Yes, it's Rod. And look, he hasn't spoken to me, not really, since Thanksgiving, so I don't even know if he cares or if I'm imagining things. But if I can unravel this whole mess I've made, I'm going to find out."

Lisa made a dismissive sound with her lips. "Jesus, Travis. I wish I smoked. You are seriously messed up."

"I'm really sorry for hurting you."

"Well, I'm glad I dodged a bullet. I don't think being bi is your problem, Travis. Your problem is, you're a coward."

That stung.

He stood up and headed toward the door. There wasn't much more he could say, and he'd offered his sincere apology.

"Have a great trip, Lisa. Do all the things you've wanted to. I'll see you around."

He thought he heard her mutter, "Not if I see you first" as he shut the door behind him, but he didn't care.

.   .   .

Now Travis was really at loose ends. Things with Lisa were truly over, but he didn't know what to do about Rod, Walla Walla, wheat farming—basically his entire life. He was no longer engaged, true, but there was a gaping hole where his future had once been. At least he'd known what that future was. And it wasn't as if he could call Rod for advice.

The only person he told was Abigail, when he was able to catch her on the phone between her classes and her various study groups.

"She really tried to pepper spray you?"

"Yeah. I'm surprised Mom and Dad didn't hear anything."

"Now what?"

Travis acted like he didn't know what... or who... she was referring to. "Now what, what?"

He knew she was rolling her eyes by the tone of her voice. "You broke it off—and I'm glad—but now what are you going to do? What does Rod think about the whole mess?"

Now it was Travis's turn to roll his eyes. She had a one-track mind. "Good lord, Abs, how would I know? We've talked maybe three times since Thanksgiving."

"Ah, so I was right!"

"Right about what?"

"Duh, right that Rod has feelings for you and is off licking his wounds."

"Abs..."

"Fine, you still have your head in the sand. Or maybe somewhere darker, like up your butt."

"Abs, I can't talk about this, I gotta go."

His dad seemed to understand that Travis needed to be kept busy: suddenly there was a lot more work than usual for this time of year. Michael even paid for Travis to attend a seminar on agribusiness and the global market. Travis looked forward to both the seminar and getting out of Walla Walla, even if it was only to Phoenix.

He and his dad were out driving the property, doing maintenance and generally checking that things were ready for spring. Then his dad stopped at the John Deere dealership to look at some fancy machinery and shoot the breeze with the franchise owner. One thing Travis did like about his home town was that even big business was still small.

While he waited, Travis chatted with John Briggs, a guy he'd gone to middle and high school with. In Walla Walla, unless you were Catholic or Seventh-day Adventist, everyone went to the same public high school. Tractor talk was pretty far down on the list of things Travis enjoyed, but as soon as his dad and the owner were out of earshot, John changed the subject.

"So I heard from my mom that you and Lisa Harris got engaged." John waggled his eyebrows. One more reason Travis hated his hometown. Just once he'd like to be anonymous. The Walkers, due to the sheer amount of acreage they owned, were never anonymous. Even now that the small city was known for more than wheat, onions, and a maximum-security prison, most residents recognized his last name.

Travis thought he'd probably rather talk about tractors. "Yeah." He couldn't deny the statement, even if wasn't true anymore. He kind of wished Abigail hadn't brought up Rod again the other day, because now that was all he was thinking about. He wanted, needed, to tell Rod the wedding wasn't happening. He needed to see Rod in person, to see his reaction to the news before he figured out what to do next. Rod was never very good at hiding his emotions.

Abigail was right, Rod *had* saved Travis's ass over the years, and not just when they were doing stupid stuff like daring each other to eat the worm at the bottom of the tequila bottle or seeing who could jump the farthest from the roof of the big barn with their homemade parachutes.

Now Travis was seeing Rod in a different light. Not the best friend he'd known for almost all of his life. But, as—good lord, Travis could feel his face start to heat at the thought—a lover? And the one person he should be talking to about all of these conflicting feelings was three hundred miles away instead of there like he always had been.

His inner turmoil wasn't about his sexuality. No, it stemmed from changing lanes with *Rod* in mind, a possibility of Rod as his future, instead of a Lisa or Ashely or...

Travis cringed inwardly. What if this was all in his head? What if Travis was going through all this *thinking* and Rod was in Skagit meeting the guy who would be there for him instead of Travis? What if Rod wasn't responding to Travis's texts because there was some other guy in Trav's place?

Didn't that thought feel like a fucking bucket of ice water? He slept with guys all the time; how had he never noticed Rod? Because you didn't "notice" your best friend that way, that's why, he reminded himself.

Travis stared at the shiny green-and-yellow lawn tractors the dealership had on display, the thought of Rod with someone else *for real* pinging around in his head and making him slightly queasy. He was unable to meet John's curious regard. Travis was afraid of what the other man would see: that he was a monumental dick who had his head so far up his own ass he had no idea he was in love with his best friend.

Travis couldn't catch a breath and he felt sick, like he'd been sucker punched. His heart rate increased to the point where he felt more than a little off. He leaned against the display case full of toy tractors, some bright and shiny, others rusty from use and age.

He couldn't be with Rod... could he? Travis had a duty to get married and take care of the farm; *that* lesson had been pounded into him since he was a little boy. Even though he didn't want to live in Walla Walla and didn't enjoy wheat farming, he'd always known that was what he was supposed to do. It was Travis's duty to carry the Walker name into the future. If Travis wanted to be with Rod, it wasn't going be here.

"Earth to Travis. Hello? Aren't you supposed to be kind of excited about being engaged?"

Travis heard John's question but chose to ignore it. Lisa'd been gone two weeks, and he still hadn't faced his mother. Lisa was right, he was a coward. "Do you ever step back and wonder, like, how you got where you are?"

John furrowed his eyebrows. "Here? My dad owns this place."

"I mean..." What did he mean? It was usually Rod who asked too many questions about life and stuff. Travis was usually happy to let life happen. There were only so many things he actually had a say in. It occurred to Travis that John was in the same position he was. "Have you ever thought about leaving town? Doing something else?"

John stepped back around the counter and started to fuss with some paperwork. Travis couldn't read his expression. He didn't think his question was that out of line; a lot of people left town. Travis never saw himself leaving because of the farm, but it didn't mean he hadn't thought about it almost his entire life.

Finally John quit fidgeting. "What would I do, Travis? I'm a small-town hick. My dad needs me to help out here. I'm happy enough."

Funny, Travis thought, John didn't look happy or even "happy enough." When Travis saw him out drinking at the Green Lantern, John was often sitting alone at the bar. But he managed to keep that thought to himself. He was spending enough time at the Lantern himself he shouldn't throw stones.

His dad came back from looking at specs and salivating over new equipment, and the two of them headed back home. The cab of the truck was quiet as they drove along, neither feeling much like making conversation. Finally Travis couldn't stand the noise in his head any longer.

"Dad, have you ever wanted something else?"

His dad glanced at him quickly before returning his eyes to the road. "I'm old. Tell me what you're thinking; I'm not good at guessing."

Great, it ran in the family. Travis wasn't sure if that made him happy or not. He gestured out the window where, beyond the rundown fast food joints, taco trucks, gas stations, and the mall that had been built in the 1980s only to go bankrupt ten years later, the rolling hills of the Palouse were visible. Even in late winter they were sublime. He didn't hate everything about the town he'd grown up in.

"Here, this town, wheat farming... did you ever want to do something else?"

Michael let out a chuckle before answering, "For a while in high school, I wanted to go to seminary."

Travis side-eyed his dad. "We aren't Catholic."

"I didn't really want to go, but it was fun to horrify your grandparents. What are you really trying to ask, son?"

His dad was a quiet man who generally kept out of family drama, but he wasn't stupid. Travis opened his big mouth. "I'm not sure wheat farming is what I want. If this town is what I want."

"Is this wedding jitters or something more?" Michael pulled to a stop at a red light, patiently waiting for Travis's answer.

"I don't know, Dad, it's a lot of things. I guess I have a lot of thinking to do."

"Well, that's a first."

Travis stared at his dad, who started to chuckle. "You've got that conference next week. Maybe that'll help."

The light turned green, and Michael accelerated across the intersection. Maybe the time away *would* help. The rest of the ride was made in comfortable silence, Travis watching the town he'd known all his life flicker past, wondering if he wanted it to be his future... and if he didn't, what he was going to do about it.

## 5

**R**od stared at the notification on his screen. TheoG1988 wanted to know more about him.

*Great.* The thought rolled around in his head, dripping with sarcasm.

Really, it *was* great. He was never going to meet someone if he rolled his eyes every time an email or text came through. At least TheoG1988 had sent him an actual email and not started with a dick pic. Rod liked dick as much as the next gay guy, but he really wasn't interested in seeing some stranger's parts before they even met.

He found it disturbing to arrange to meet a guy and know what his dick looked like, but not his face. Was he supposed to ask for proof when they met up? Grab their crotch? Compare the real thing to the picture? It was all very confusing.

Another email came in while Rod was contemplating answering TheoG1988. It was from Travis, of course. Somehow he managed to remind Rod he existed, even when they were miles apart.

Travis was at some conference in Phoenix for three days. Out of the blue, he'd sent Rod a couple bare-chested selfies with the city sprawled out behind him in the desert. It had been quiet between them since just after Thanksgiving. Rod struggled between appreciating that Travis had read and understood the note he'd left about needing space, and desperately missing his best friend. Rod stared at the image on his phone. Travis looked tired, and he'd lost his summer tan. Was his smile a little forced?

There was, according to Travis's text, only one hill there big enough to climb, and he was headed out to climb it the next morning. He promised more pictures. Gah. Rod had no desire to go to Phoenix, not really, but it looked more appealing if Travis was there.

And... he deleted TheoG1988's message, because clearly he wasn't ready to date. At all. Maybe he would move to some remote mountain range and live off the land. Or something. Tossing his phone onto the couch cushion next to him, he slumped backward, resting his head against the back of the couch.

Travis aside, Rod was worried about Jasper Ransom. He didn't think the kid had changed his clothes—or at the very least laundry hadn't been done in his household—in weeks. Jasper also often didn't have lunch with him, his backpack sitting far too flat against his narrow back. The lunch lady, as Karen Browning laughingly called herself, would never deny a hungry kid a meal, but even she probably had some sort of free-lunch limit she couldn't cross.

Earlier that day, when Rod had been parked in his spot for after-school pickup, she'd stopped and talked to him before heading to her car.

"Hi, Bus Driver Rod." She snickered.

"Lunch Lady Karen." Funny how he'd known what she wanted to talk to him about.

"Question." She looked around, apparently making sure there were no close ears. "Have you seen an adult with Jasper

Ransom? I'm a little concerned about him. Since the holiday break he hasn't had lunch money put in his account, and I'm pretty sure he's wearing the same clothing. There's been a sub in his classroom who's barely holding it together, so he may not have noticed Jasper's issues."

Anxiety snaked through Rod's stomach. He'd hoped he was imagining it. But no, it seemed that something was going on with Jasper after all.

"I haven't. He's never come to the stop with anyone. Have you asked him?"

"I have, kind of, but he has the attention span of a gnat, and I didn't want to make him feel uncomfortable. Plus, I'm only the lunch lady. I'll say something to Principal Snow if you think there's cause."

INSTEAD OF SETTING himself up for an excruciating date with a stranger, Rod would do a little detective work. He'd drive the part of the route where he picked Jasper up and see if he could find anything out. What he might find out by merely driving down a street, he had no idea... but it was better than sitting on the couch staring into space. Wondering what Travis was doing in Phoenix.

Rod's bus route ran circuitously around the northeast edge of Skagit. There were fourteen elementary schools in Skagit, and Yew, where Jasper went, was one with some of the most economically challenged students. The street he meandered down had a defeated feel to it, as if residents had given up the fight, or at least not many had the time or money to paint their houses and fix up their yards.

These houses had all been built post–World War II, probably to meet the demand of returning soldiers and their expanding families. Some looked like they hadn't been painted since then. As his truck rumbled along, Rod tried to find some kind of sign of Jasper. He'd done a little research on the name Ransom before he left his apartment but hadn't found any addresses with that name, at least not in that neighborhood.

The fact that it was already dark at six p.m. didn't help matters, but Rod needed to be out doing something. Anything. Looking for where Jasper might live was at least less useless than sitting around wondering about Travis. About how the wedding plans were going. The few times they'd talked, Rod had come up with excuses to end the call before the subject came up. He didn't even know if Travis and Lisa had set a date yet. Rod was pretty sure Lenore Walker wouldn't let the engagement linger too long.

And there he was, thinking about Travis again. God fucking dammit.

Stepping sharply on the brake, Rod swung his truck around and headed toward downtown. He might as well stop by the Loft and see if Cam was working. Maybe a beer or two would help him loosen up a bit and write a decent reply to TheoG1988.

Far too late for the time he had to be at work in the morning, Rod stumbled home to his apartment. He pulled TheoG1988's message out of the trash and replied before he fell asleep on the couch with all the lights on.

JASPER MADE it to the bus stop the next morning. He didn't look much better than Rod felt. His clothes were rumpled, and Rod could see where he'd spilled something, ketchup maybe, on his shirt. One shoe was untied, and his backpack was again empty of anything resembling a lunch. What was going on?

"Hey, little guy, how's it going?"

"Okay." Jasper didn't say anything else before he went to sit in his seat directly behind Rod. He didn't even ask what part of the story they were working on during the rest of the ride.

Before pulling away from the curb, Rod quickly glanced behind him. Jasper was staring out the window. Rod wanted to ask him again if everything was all right. Instead, he flicked off the "No Passing" blinkers and pulled out into Skagit morning traffic.

## 6

T ravis rolled out of bed, his head throbbing. He'd been at the Lantern until closing the night before. No doubt his dad wasn't going to be impressed. At least it was still winter *and* Travis wasn't sixteen anymore, so his dad's decades-old threat of making him move the woodpile (by hand) from one side of the yard to the other had no effect.

He stared blearily at the contents of his closet, trying to decide what stupid T-shirt he was going to wear with his jeans, when a memory from one of the first times he'd gotten drunk popped into his head. One summer during high school, he and Rod had "found" a partially empty fifth of Jack Daniel's. Boy, Travis hadn't thought about that in a long, long time. They'd driven way out on Cottonwood Road to a semi-abandoned property a few miles from town and sat in the back of Travis's pickup truck trading the bottle back and forth until suddenly it was empty.

Even though he'd been very drunk at the time, Travis remembered with absolute clarity looking down to see Rod's hand on his leg. He'd watched, somewhat disassociated, as Rod gently ran his fingers up and down the exposed skin, tracing a scar left over from something stupid they'd done, the work-roughened skin on Rod's palm catching the hairs on Travis's thigh.

Travis had known that they were both drunk, and maybe Rod more than him because Rod was smaller. But as the heat beat down on them, heating the metal bed of the truck underneath their asses and making him feel loose and languid, all Travis knew was that he really needed Rod to slide his hand closer to Travis's groin: he needed Rod to touch him. His body was aware and onboard with the idea of those slim fingers wrapping around his cock and stroking him until he came. He'd let his own hand slip on top of Rod's, guiding him gently to where Travis wanted to feel it.

With his other hand, he'd unbuttoned his shorts and pulled them open as much as he could, pushing his underwear down, sitting awkwardly back against the cab of the truck and allowing his knees to fall to the sides. Rod's eyes widened when Travis's fully erect cock made its appearance, and Travis had thought he might stop, but instead Rod wrapped his hand around him and began to pump. Uncertainly at first, watching Travis to see if he was doing it right, and then with more confidence as Travis hardened further in his hand. Regardless of the whiskey, it probably only took about two minutes before Travis's balls clenched and he watched, fascinated, as come began pulsing from his cock and he rutted into Rod's hand wanting more, another wave of desire surging through him.

They'd passed out about then and woken up hours later sunburned and hella thirsty, the sky overhead lit by a million stars instead of the blazing sun. Neither ever mentioned what'd happened between them; when they woke up they both acted like nothing happened. Travis wondered if Rod remembered. Had it meant something more than that they were two horny teenagers? Travis was officially too stupid to live, because it meant something to *him*, even if he had pushed it to the back of his mind for far too long.

Now what was he going to do? When you're hungover and dealing with the realization that you love someone, always loved that someone but called it something else—are you allowed a do-over? After all these years, Travis knew, he *already* loved Rod. The other guys, the women, *Lisa*, they were him being blind to what he already had. He deserved it if Rod had given up on him.

He grabbed the first shirt he saw and a reasonably clean pair of jeans before sitting back down on his bed. What a fucking loser he was.

THE NIGHT BEFORE, John Briggs had shown up at the tavern and the two of them ended up drinking bourbon with beer backs, comparing how their lives in town sucked. Travis had been spending most of his free time at the bar, ignoring his dad's raised eyebrows in the mornings and his mother's "tsk"ing and judgmental sniffs. Travis wished Abs was home, even if she always fought with Lenore when she was around.

"So what's Rod up to these days? Haven't seen him in a while." John had shaken the ice down in his glass before taking another sip.

Travis was sick of answering that question. Everyone wondered where Rod was. When he told them Rod had moved away, he got a variety of responses, but they all boiled down to "What? You two are always together!"

John leaned closer in, and Travis instinctively mimicked the movement. "I always thought you guys had a thing."

"A thing?" Was Travis the only person who had no idea that Rod... He let the thought go unfinished.

"Yeah." John dropped his voice lower, his eyes darting around the half-empty tavern. "I've always been jealous you guys were able to pull it off without getting caught. A small town like ours... it's hard being gay."

Travis stiffened, letting that last sentence roll around in his head. Had John just outed himself to Trav? God, he was such shit at this. This was exactly why—well, one of the reasons why—he needed Rod. Rod would know what to do and say in this situation. Travis was bound to stick his foot in his mouth, maybe his entire leg. Instead of responding, he took a huge swig of bourbon. The remaining ice slid from the bottom of the glass, hitting him in the face as he was breathing in, and he spewed the liquid over the table and partially onto John's shirt.

When he stopped coughing up bourbon and the sting in his throat died down, he signaled the bartender for another drink. She quickly plopped a fresh pour in front of him. Travis eyed John. His shoulders were hunched, and he kept his gaze on the table, or at least somewhere to the left of Travis. Jeez, he was more freaked out about the topic than Travis was.

"To answer the first question about Rod, he's still in Skagit. I haven't seen him in a while, not since Thanksgiving." He'd been trying not to do the math, but nearly three months was a long time.

"That's gotta be some sort of record." Now John was watching Travis intently. Travis wanted to groan. Even he knew that somehow his answer here was vital, more than just his feeling of loyalty to his family, to the onus of the farm and inheritance his mother always talked about.

"Yeah. To answer your second question, Rod and I don't have a thing." Right now. As soon as Travis had everything squared away, there was going to be a "thing." Hopefully.

"Because you got engaged," John said flatly. "That's a sucky thing to do. Anyone with eyes could see the guy was totally into you. Or, well," he shrugged and looked back down into his own drink, "I could see it. Maybe other folks bought the whole 'best friend' thing."

Travis took another healthy swig of his drink, managing to get it down this time.

John was staring at him. "Are you *just* figuring this out?"

On the way home he'd tried calling Rod, but the phone went to voicemail.

HIS PHONE WAS LYING on the nightstand. He picked it up. No messages. He called his sister.

"Hey, Abs."

"Big brother," Abigail greeted him. "How's it going?"

"Could be better."

"Dad said you've been," she paused, "a bit tense."

Travis lay back down on the bed and watched the ceiling fan rotate.

"What else did he say?" He wondered if Michael had told Abigail that Travis didn't want to stay in Walla Walla.

"Not much. You know Dad's not one for a lot of conversation, especially over the phone."

"You and Dad are close." Travis stated it as fact. Even though he had never really thought about it before, he realized it was true. Abigail and Michael had a close relationship.

"Yeah, I guess. It's not like Mom and I get along."

"Why?" For some reason it was suddenly important to Travis that he understand. He'd never questioned the way his family worked before; he'd coasted along doing his thing. Apparently oblivious to dangerous undercurrents.

"Really, Trav? You are—were,"—she snickered—"the golden child. I mean, you could do no wrong in Mom's eyes." Travis could practically hear her grinding her teeth at his obtuseness. "I've always known she loves you best. The best I could ever do was follow behind and hope for some scraps to pick up. Once I figured that out, I started doing whatever I wanted, because it didn't matter anyway. Dad's always been pretty cool. We don't always agree, but at least he listens."

That was true. Michael was a great listener. Not that Travis had ever needed to share a lot with his dad, but he knew he could. His dad always had an open door.

"So, why'd you call?" she asked. "Not to ask why Mom and I don't get along."

"About what you said at Thanksgiving..." He let his voice trail off.

"Have you talked to Rod?"

"No. Texted a bit."

"Has Rod reached out to you? Has he called, or texted you first?"

Travis thought for a minute. "No, he hasn't done either."

Abigail's sigh was audible across the line. "Trav, I know you graduated magna cum laude—I mean, I was at your graduation —but sometimes I think there's a lot of stuff you're kind of stupid about."

"Numbers are easy," Travis muttered. They *were* easy. They stayed the same. He knew what they were going to do and how they fit in equations. In some ways numbers were easier than the alphabet, or were an extension of the alphabet.

"Yeah, and practically since you crawled out of the womb you've had Rod at your back. Plus you're lucky enough to be hot too, so you don't even have to work at having whoever you want in your bed. Most girls, or boys, don't care that you have the emotional depth of a jellyfish."

"You and I look a lot alike. And there's some pretty jellyfish." Travis thought comparing him to a jellyfish was kind of mean.

"You're beginning to give them a bad name." Abigail kind of laughed. "Trav, Rod's in love with you! He has been, I dunno how long, but probably since he figured out boys were his jam."

Travis ignored all the ridiculous metaphors Abigail rolled out, focusing on the one thing that was important. "Are you sure Rod's in love with me?"

"Yes, slowpoke brother, Rod Beton is in love with you. Or at least he *was*. I mean, the guy probably has a limit, and it could be that announcing that you and Lisa Harris were a thing was it."

"I am a jellyfish."

"You are," she agreed. "What are you going to do about it?"

Travis had some ideas. He had been thinking about how to make this whole thing work. "Well, for one thing he wasn't, isn't, talking to me, and I needed to sort some stuff out." He couldn't believe he was talking to his sister about this.

"Look, Trav, maybe you need to approach this a little differently. You're used to things just happening in your life, and they always work out. But. What is the constant in your life?"

"Like a number? A factor?"

"Yeah."

"Well, aside from family, the farm..." A circuit sprang to life, practically humming in his head. "Rod."

"Good, good, Rod is a constant. Now, what happens when a constant changes?"

Things fall apart, that's what. Travis groaned. Abigail made agreeing noises. But... "Okay, say you're right about, uh, Rod— why hasn't he said anything?"

"I don't know, Travis, maybe it's because you've been busy taking every girl and *other* boy to bed ever since you got hormones?"

And never once had Travis looked at the man who'd been at his side through it all. "I need to think about this."

Like he hadn't been already. But somehow talking to his

sister made it real. More real. Travis still didn't know *how* to do what he wanted to do. What the right thing to do was. He wasn't cut out for all this emotional stuff. Like she'd said, usually things happened and he went along with it.

Which, as he thought about it now, maybe wasn't the best approach.

"You really don't," she said. "Something tells me, brother of mine, that you have thought this to death, and now you need to get off your ass and *do* something about it."

## 7

TheoG1988 seemed like a super-nice guy. The kiss of death, right? Nobody wanted to be the "super-nice guy." After exchanging texts, they decided to meet up at the Skagit citizens' favorite for coffee and lunch. Rod spotted the self-described skinny-as-fuck hyperactive eurotrash right away. They got off to a good start when Theo confessed to Rod that he was terrified of meeting a stranger online.

"I promised myself I would give it the old schoolboy try, but I'm not sure if I'm cut out to meet people online. Ugh, meeting up with someone with the expectation of like..." he waved a hand between them, "you know."

Rod laughed. He did know. He'd definitely hooked up with guys for the sole purpose of sex, but it had always been awkward, and as soon as the edge was off he couldn't get away fast enough. One time he'd left without tying his shoes. "Me too."

Theo was the exact opposite, physically, of Travis, and he made no attempt to hide that he was gay. Rod rolled his eyes at himself. He didn't hide that he was gay, either, but it couldn't be denied that most straight people never caught on to his sexuality. As a teen he'd been glad to fit in, but now he wondered if "fitting in" meant denying a part of himself.

Theo was a freelance photographer and blogger. He was working on a personal piece about migrant workers, immigration, and identity. He'd only moved to Skagit from Denver a few months earlier than Rod.

"My great-grandparents came to the US from Portugal. I want to understand why people are still coming, what is still better about here, the US. I want to explore work and employment and pride. My greats were never ashamed of their journey, not for one second. I'm following their immigration trail, I guess, and trying to compare it to today's."

"And here I drive a school bus and can't decide what I want to do with my life." Rod's English degree was gathering dust somewhere in the bottom of a box. At least he'd paid off the last of his student loans after the last season of firefighting. Travis had done what his parents wanted, gotten an ag degree, and excelled in it like he had everything.

"What did you do before you moved to Skagit?"

"My buddy Travis and I worked for the Forest Service as firefighters for the past four summers. After college I worked as a veterinarian's assistant for a while." Rod had really liked working for Dr. Mortimer and had harbored a tiny crush on him. It would be difficult for anyone not to find the ginger doctor with his soft West Virginia accent attractive. More than once, Rod had watched women swoon when he came into the exam room to examine their pets.

"Oh my god, you fight fires *and* you save the animals?" Theo pretend-swooned.

"Well, now that you put it that way..." Rod chuckled. "But I couldn't get into actual vet school, so I got an English degree. And then when I graduated I wanted to pay off my loans, so really not all that altruistic."

Theo shook his head. "I don't know, I can totally imagine you on one of those sexy firefighter calendars, holding a puppy in one hand and a romance novel in the other. Oh, and in front of a shiny clean red-hot fire engine. That is a calendar I would keep way after the year ended."

He fanned himself, and Rod couldn't help but laugh again.

While they chatted, the coffee shop hummed, buzzed, and whistled around them. Police officers from the station across the street came in, ordering coffees and pastries before heading back out to their desks or patrol cars. A handsome but grim-looking man wearing a suit and carrying a briefcase entered and stood for a second looking around before coming and sitting at the table next to them. A few minutes later he was joined by a taller man casually dressed in worn jeans and a cozy sweater, with a coffee drink from the counter in either hand. His hair was a mass of wild curls that he blew out of his face with a puff of air. He set the coffees down before leaning over and whispering something in the suit's ear that Rod couldn't catch.

Suit smiled then, his face changing from grim to something approaching soft, and it became abundantly clear to Rod that the two men were a couple. An ache that had nothing to do with the current flu virus going around town throbbed in his chest.

Theo was cute and funny, Rod couldn't deny it. He was slender, his complexion darker than Rod's own. His black hair was cut short, with longer bangs that he kept having to sweep away from his face, and he talked wildly with his hands, twice nearly sending their coffees flying off the small table. And he seemed genuinely interested in Rod.

"So, uh," Theo glanced up from fiddling with his coffee spoon, "would you want to get dinner sometime?" They'd been talking for long enough that Rod's coffee had gotten cold and the lunch rush had died away.

There was no reason for him not to say yes. Travis's image

flashed across his mind, but Rod brushed it away. "Sounds great."

They made a date for that Friday, and Rod was amazed that he found himself looking forward to seeing Theo again.

THE NEXT MORNING Jasper missed the bus. Rod waited as long as he could, but the other kids couldn't be late to school because Rod had waited for one child. After the kids trooped off, Rod making sure that everyone remembered their backpacks and lunches, coats and sweaters, he pulled the bus around to the parking lot and made his way to the principal's office.

Why was it that all schools smelled the same? Yew Elementary was an older three-story brick building, the administrative offices located just past the front doors. Rod quickly found the principal's office inside another room, with an assistant or secretary's desk guarding entrance. A middle-aged woman was answering the phone while looking at her computer screen. A few parents were already waiting patiently.

When it was finally his turn, Rod introduced himself and explained that he was one of the bus drivers.

"Ah, you must be Bus Driver Rod," the assistant said cheerfully, her smile bright, bouncing dreadlocks barely restrained by a fuchsia headband. "We've heard a ton about you. What can I help you with?"

"Well, I'm not really sure." Rod launched into how he and the lunch lady were worried about Jasper—about his seeming lack of hygiene and how he didn't have lunch money, and today he hadn't been at the bus stop.

"Some of our kids have it pretty hard. I'm sure you understand I can't give out any personal information, but I can take down what you've shared and let Principal Snow know."

"I'm really worried that he missed school today." Rod didn't know how to get her to understand that Jasper seemed to come to school *because* of the bus and the stories they were all working on. Missing an installment was not something the third-grader would do lightly.

"I'll pass it along, I promise."

With that assurance and no other recourse, Rod stepped back out into the misty morning. Once he dropped the bus back at the lot, he drove the route again, winding up and down the streets in the vicinity of Jasper's stop but seeing nothing more than he had before. An economically depressed neighborhood, ill-kept yards, cars that had sat in one spot so long there was moss growing on the roofs. Residents working hard to keep their heads above water. But no sign of a grubby nine-year-old boy with a wild imagination who preferred wearing his coat as a superhero cloak.

FINALLY IT WAS FRIDAY, and his date with Theo loomed. They'd texted once since their coffee date, Theo making sure that Rod was still coming. They were meeting up at the Loft, a place Rod was regretting suggesting, but he didn't feel like he could tell Theo that. The last thing Rod needed was Cam giving him a hard time about being on a date. Ah well.

The bar was busy, but the side with tables had space for the two of them. Rod didn't recognize the new guy checking ID at the door, but he did recognize Cam's familiar form behind the bar. His friend had his long hair tucked up in a messy bun. Rod did not know a single other man who could pull that off, but on Cameron it was sexy. Thankfully Cam was too busy making drinks and entertaining to see Rod come in with his date.

During the entire meal, Rod kept trying to force the spark, the physical attraction toward Theo. Clearly Theo was into Rod; he kept leaning forward while they were talking, putting his hand on Rod's forearm and quickly removing it. Their knees bumped, and Rod was pretty sure it wasn't by accident. He supposed it was the wrong attitude to be gearing up for the inevitable kiss.

Theo wanted to dance, and it was impossible for Rod to say no. The dance floor was packed with most of the gay population of Skagit dancing and grinding the night away. A song came on that Rod recognized but couldn't name, and Theo grabbed his hand and pulled him into the throng. He was a good dancer, much better than Rod. He definitely got the attention of other dancers. He was one of those guys who seemed to innately know the beat and be able to respond in exact time with the song. Rod did his thing where he kind of stood in one place and moved his hips around a bit.

"Did I mention I am a terrible dancer?" he shouted over the music.

Theo grinned. "No worries, I'll make up for it. You just stay right there and look sexy as hell."

Soon enough another, better dancer swept Theo away, taking him deeper onto the dance floor. Rod let him go without a single spark of jealousy. He made his way off the dance floor and wandered over to the bar where Cameron was still pouring drinks, a second bartender backing him up now.

"Hey, Rod, I didn't see you come in!" Cam grinned at him. Rod sure hoped Ira knew how lucky he was.

"I'm with a date."

Cam stopped shaking the drink in progress to stare at Rod. "A date? Really?"

"Yes, really."

He started shaking the drink again. "Where is he, then?"

Rod looked back out across the dance floor. It took him a minute before dancers moved and he was able to spot Theo dancing between two other men. Rod didn't know either of them, but as he watched, the one dancing behind slid his hand up Theo's shirt, and Rod saw Theo freeze.

"There, with red shirt guy and tall frowny guy." Red shirt guy now had his fingers wrapped around Theo's hip and was grinding against him. Theo had started dancing again, but he didn't look nearly as carefree as he had before.

Red shirt put his arms around Theo, forcing the smaller man back against him. Rod saw Theo try to squirm away, but Red kept a firm grip on him.

Cameron followed Rod's gaze. "Shit, it's that asshole. Sterling eighty-sixed him; how'd he get back in? Go get your friend." Cam signaled to the bouncer, pointing at the dance floor just as Theo jabbed his elbow into Red's abdomen and stomped on his foot at the same time.

When Rod reached Theo's side, he didn't bother to ask— neither had red shirt guy, but based on Theo's attentiveness during dinner, Rod felt confident his touch was more welcome — he just took Theo's forearm and pulled him away from the other two men.

"What the fuck is going on here? When a guy says no, you need to listen." Rod had to raise his voice to be heard above the pounding music.

The bouncer joined them, and the other men dancing moved away.

"We were just dancing." Red shirt had a tone that Rod didn't like.

"It didn't look like dancing, and it didn't look like my date was having fun."

Frowny guy stepped between them. "Baby, we'll find another."

Rod didn't care what kind of games those two were involved in. He turned his back on them, letting the bouncer sort the rest out and guiding Theo back toward the bar.

"You okay? Sorry I left, nobody wants to dance with a clumsy lunk, and I thought you were having fun."

Theo smiled up at him, but some of the spark had disappeared from his expression. "Yeah, I love to dance. I was having fun until that asshole started mauling me. You're not a bad dancer." He poked Rod in the biceps. "You just need more practice."

Rod snorted. "Tell that to everybody I ever knocked down with my fancy moves. Can I buy you a drink to make up for it?" He waggled his eyebrows suggestively.

As intended, Theo laughed, but he still declined. "I think I'm ready to go home. Sorry. I do love to dance—it's that asshole who ruined my night, not you."

Rod walked Theo to his car a couple of blocks away and waited as Theo disarmed the alarm. Theo turned to face him and stepped closer so that Rod was looking down into his nearly black eyes. Lifting up on his toes, Theo pressed his lips against Rod's. The kiss was over before Rod could react. Theo slid behind the wheel of his car with a soft "See you soon," before starting the engine and heading down the street.

BECAUSE HIS BRAIN was apparently broken, or like a scratched vinyl record stuck in the same spot, the erotic dream Rod had that night did not star TheoG1988. It was Travis's blond head he was looking at while lips traced up and down his erection, Travis's blue eyes that looked at him full of mischief and daring while he sucked Rod further down. Rod felt himself hit the back of Travis's throat, and it was the most incredible sensation. He thrust harder, wanting more. Wanting not to be inside Travis but Travis to be inside him.

Rod was on his stomach then, lifting his hips up so Travis could take him. Take him like he wanted so badly. He felt when

Travis propped his knees under Rod's ass and began to trace his exposed hole with his finger. Rod's hand was around his cock, precome dripping onto the sheet beneath him, but all he cared about was not coming too soon. At least not before Travis put his fingers inside him.

So much teasing. "Please, please, please," Rod chanted.

"Please what? You want me to fuck you or make love to you?" Travis rasped, his voice smoky with lust and need.

"Fuck me, love me, both. All." Rod sobbed as fingers pushed their way inside, his ass reflexively clenching before he relaxed and pushed back against the intruders. Welcomed them.

"You want my cock yet? Can you take it? I want you to feel me all day, to never forget me."

Rod had seen Travis naked plenty of times, but only once with an erection that he remembered. His dream brain managed to fill in the blanks just fine, though.

"I want everything, anything you can give me." He was moaning and making a complete fool of himself, and then Travis's fingers were rubbing back and forth across his prostate and nothing else mattered. Not even the fact that this was a dream and Rod knew it.

WHEN HE WOKE in the morning, there was a missed call from Travis. Without thinking about it, he hit return call. Trav picked up right away.

"You're hard to get ahold of, dude, what have you been up to?"

Before his sleepy brain could filter his answer, words popped out. "I was out last night. We went to dinner, stayed out a little late."

Travis was silent for a beat. Rod wondered what he was

thinking, if he was relieved that Rod appeared to have met someone.

"Oh yeah? What's his name? How did you meet him?"

"Theo, his name is Theo. We met through a dating app."

Travis's voice was stern. "A dating app? You're better than that. He could be any kind of creep."

"He's not a creep, Travis. He's a nice guy, a photographer, and he's new to Skagit like me. We hit it off."

Rod didn't really intend to mislead Travis about the possibility of a relationship between him and Theo, but it was important for Travis to know Rod was making a new life for himself in Skagit.

"If things work out, I'll have a plus one for your big day. Do you guys have a date and all that? A best man needs to know these things." God, it was hard. Rod didn't want think about having to watch Travis get married, hearing him say to another person the words Rod wanted to hear for himself.

Silence. Rod wondered if the connection had been lost.

"Trav? You there?"

There was a muffled curse and thump. Travis must have dropped the phone. Finally he answered.

"Hang on, sorry. Yeah, about that... Lisa... uh, yeah, anyway. So, uh... shit." There were more thumps and a scuffling sound. What was he doing? "Sorry. Hey, did you catch the game the other night?"

They talked for a little while longer, Travis giving Rod crap about his losing college basketball team, but the conversation felt forced. They hung up with a mutual "Great to talk to you, see you soon" kind of thing. Rod dropped his phone beside him on the bed and shut his eyes. As he lay there, he wondered if it had been his imagination that Travis's enthusiasm for his upcoming wedding had seemed flat or if it was just the inevitable changing of their friendship.

He and Travis would no longer call each other when their stupid sports teams lost or won. They wouldn't know the minutiae of each other's lives—if they'd been sick, had a bad day, or stayed up too late binge-watching a new show—because they were no longer around each other to witness them. It was already happening.

A heaviness Rod vaguely recognized as grief pressed him further down into the mattress. He could lie there, and the oppressive weight of it would force all the tears he'd never shed, all the love he'd never been able to give, from his body, leaving him only a husk.

He stayed in bed all day, turning off his cell phone so he wouldn't have to talk to anyone. When the sun set, he didn't bother turning the lights on.

---

## 8

Travis viciously slapped white paint onto the wall of the storage room. Excess paint dripped downward; splatters that looked like constellations bloomed where the roller had hit the wall. His dad had been complaining that it was too dingy to see their inventory. This bright white should take care of that.

After talking to Rod that morning, he finished dressing, grabbed his keys from the bowl on the kitchen counter, and left the house, ignoring his mother's demand that he stop and talk to her. No one ignored Lenore. The expression on her face would have been priceless if Travis were in any mood to laugh. Why hadn't he just *told* Rod he and Lisa were off? That there were no marriage plans?

The fucking wedding. Travis slapped more paint on the wall. The wedding both he and Lisa knew wasn't happening. The only people left to tell who mattered were his parents and Rod. Rod, Rod, Rod. Surely Lisa's dad already knew. She wouldn't go on a long trip with him and not say anything. Right?

And Rod. Although, Travis smacked another roller full of

paint onto the wall, from what Rod had said on the phone, it could be too late. While Travis was fucking around trying to figure out up from down, Rod had met someone else. Someone named Theo who was "a nice guy." But it wasn't too late to be honest with himself, his family, and Rod.

How stupid to create a separation. Rod was family. Travis's family.

"There's more paint on the floor than the wall, son."

Travis whipped around, the roller still in his hand, barely managing to jerk backward before smacking his dad in the chest.

"A little on edge, are you? Your mother is furious, claimed you stomped out of the house."

Travis carefully placed the paint roller in the aluminum pan before answering. "I did." He crossed his arms over his chest defensively, ready for an argument with Michael.

"You want to go for a drive?" Michael looked at the paint and the mess Travis had made. "This can be cleaned up later—and it already looks brighter in here. The extra paint on the floor is a nice added touch."

Travis narrowed his eyes. His dad was... making a joke? Was it possible? Michael wasn't known for his sense of humor. He wasn't mean, he just didn't interact with Travis or Abigail that way. Throughout Travis's childhood, Michael had been a strong and silent, sort of shadowy, figure. Up early and out late working the property or meeting with other farmers or planning out the next year or two, he'd left the parenting to Lenore. He'd been at Travis's sporting events when he could manage, and once Travis (and Rod) were old enough to be more of a help than a hindrance they spent time with his dad learning the ropes of the business, but they never casually joked around.

"Sure, yeah, I can go for a drive. Where're we going?"

. . .

THEY WERE both quiet at first as Michael directed his truck toward Stateline. He'd muttered something about special parts while Travis cleaned up the paint mess as best he could. The silence wasn't awkward, but it felt full. There was something waiting to be said, and it was about time.

Michael spoke first.

"I'm worried about you, Travis. You seem down, different. Not what I'd expect from someone who has a wedding coming up."

Trust the silent one to cut to the heart of the issue. Travis looked out the window, watching as trees and houses he'd seen all his life flashed past. Travis didn't see them. He could have said where they were, though; he didn't need to look out the window to know that.

The truth came spilling out. In the cab of the truck with the road winding out in front and behind them, it suddenly seemed easy to say what had been wearing him down for weeks. Months.

"Lisa and I aren't getting married. I broke it off before she left."

His dad made a noise that in Michael Walker–speak meant "Keep talking."

The moment was like what Travis imagined in near-death experiences when people claimed their life flashed before their eyes. The road behind him was the way his life had been: planned out by his parents, his community, and even himself before he knew who he was, sprawled a tangled spool of thread. College, wheat, marriage, kids. Ahead, Travis's future was largely unknown, another spool, hidden from sight the way a wispy bank of morning fog blanketed the road ahead of the truck. The truth was on the other side of that fog, just a sketch, indeterminate but beckoning. If Travis didn't head toward the truth, he would find himself in the same lonely place as John Briggs, as any of the other unhappy people who stayed in place instead of following their dream.

Travis stared fixedly out the windshield as he spoke. Maybe then it wouldn't be so hard to get the words out. Surely his dad wouldn't stop the truck and make him walk home. "The thing is," he breathed out quickly, "I'm bi, and Rod is the one I want to be with. He's the one I want, not Lisa. If he ever speaks to me again. I messed up, Dad, and I think I really hurt him."

Of course he'd also hurt Lisa, and he was about to hurt his mom; probably his dad too. He was leaving a trail of hurt in his wake. How had it come to this? He didn't like hurting people.

He was afraid to look over at his dad. The road flashed by solid and real, trees and houses all the same, the sun shining somewhere. The truck hadn't slowed, maintaining a steady speed as they headed toward wherever it was they were going.

"I'm afraid I haven't been a very good parent to you and Abigail." His dad's voice was full of sadness.

Travis about snapped his head off, jerking around to stare at his dad. "What are you talking about? You've been a great parent."

"Travis." It was his dad this time staring fixedly out the windshield. "You're twenty-eight years old, and only now are you telling me this." His dad let out a big sigh, then took a hand from the steering wheel to quickly grip Travis's thigh. "I know I'm of a different generation and a small-town man, but we've lost too many of our kids because of judging who makes them happiest. I don't like seeing you like this, Travis. I want you to be happy."

Travis thought he'd done a pretty good job hiding his emotions, but apparently even his dad, who he'd thought was allergic to emotion, had noticed his misery.

"Also, Dad, I think... I don't want to stay here, in town." He had to force the words out, but he'd said it. Admitting he didn't want to be a part of the family business was *almost* harder than confessing his sexuality. He wanted to vomit.

Jesus fucking Christ, being a grownup was hard.

"I know, son, I've seen that too. You're good at farming, but your heart isn't. You're one of those people who... well, I can't say I'm surprised, but it does make things complicated." His dad let out another deep sigh. "Your mother won't take this well."

"I'm sorry." Travis didn't know what else to say.

"You know, the parcel out behind the Bakers' property is yours. Your grandmother left it to you."

The parcel of land his dad was talking about was nineteen acres and hilly. Extra hilly. All the land around Walla Walla was rolling hills, but that particular piece seemed to have a lot of them. A stream ran along one edge, and Travis held the water rights, which was unusual these days.

"What are you saying? That I should sell it?"

Michael waggled his head noncommittally. "Maybe you should see what your options are. Before you sort that out, though, maybe you should sort out what's going on with Rod. I've always liked that boy. If things work out for you, he's going to have his hands full." Michael chuckled.

Travis pretend-glowered at his dad. "Hey, I'm not that bad," he protested with little weight behind the words.

"You just keep believing that, son."

"You're really okay with all this?"

Michael was quiet for a while, but it wasn't the kind of quiet that made Travis squirm. This was his dad thinking.

"Yes, son. I love you just as I love Abigail. I want you to be happy."

An uneasy thought made itself known. He wasn't sure how to say it, much less to his dad. Yet Travis felt it was now or never, in this truth-saying between him and Michael.

"I'm, um, worried about telling Mom." Worried was an understatement. When Rod had come out, freshman year of college, Lenore had responded to the news with a staunch "No child of mine" attitude. She'd even tried to tell Travis Rod wasn't coming to the house anymore. Michael had put a stop to that with a quiet, "Don't be ridiculous, Lenore," and things had continued mostly as they always had.

"We'll see, son, we'll see." Michael tapped the steering wheel with his thumb.

DINNER WAS ready and waiting on the dining room table when they arrived at home. It was quiet with just the three of them, but tonight the quiet felt oppressive to Travis. Anxiety about the upcoming conversation with Lenore kept him from eating much. His dad winked at him, which made him feel about eight years old again and gearing up to confess that he'd put that dead snake in Abigail's bed.

"Aren't you hungry, Travis?" Lenore asked.

"Ate a late lunch," Travis lied.

"I certainly hope you didn't stop at one of those Mexican trucks. Do you think you ate something bad?"

"Mom, I'm fine." These days it seemed everything his mother said had an off cast to it, one he'd not paid attention to before. Like people didn't get food poisoning at the county fair every year.

Finally dinner was finished, and his mom started to gather up the dishes. Travis tried to help her, but she swatted him away, telling him it was her job. He rolled his eyes at her. His mom had a lot of ideas about who did what in a household. If she wanted to do the dishes and cook, he wasn't going to argue, but... it didn't have to be that way. Travis was perfectly happy doing the dishes.

"Don't argue with her, son, it's not worth it," his dad said.

It used to crack Rod up when Michael called the both of them "son." "I don't think he knows my real name," Rod would say.

"He doesn't always call us 'son.' Sometimes he calls us 'little bastards,'" Travis had reminded him.

Travis snagged a beer from the fridge, attempting to stay out of his mom's way as she organized the dirty dishes to her liking. When she was done, she'd come into the TV room for a little while, like she always did before heading to bed, where she'd watch TV that wasn't sports. A basketball game was playing on the TV in the family room. Travis plopped onto the big blue corduroy couch with a sigh. His dad sat to the side in a matching easy chair. Travis thought both pieces of furniture were ugly, but no one had asked his opinion.

It was a good game. His team had a run at getting into the championships, and the guys were playing hard. Travis zoned out watching the players run up and down the court making impossible shots and breaking his heart when the ball went wide or short. He wondered if Rod was watching.

He hated wondering and not just knowing—because Rod should be with him, he knew that now. They should be watching the games together. It wasn't normal to be wondering what he was doing and... Travis had been avoiding thinking the name... if *Theo* was watching the game with Rod in Travis's stead. Sitting in Travis's spot next to Rod.

The clatter coming from the kitchen was tapering off, and with a sinking feeling in his stomach, Travis figured it was now or never. Telling his mom the wedding was off *and* he was bi wasn't going to get any easier. He couldn't go to Skagit without knowing his future was his own, that he'd cleared the slate. Hopefully not too late.

He sat up and put his empty beer bottle on the end table, accidentally bumping the land line phone off the hook. His folks would never consider having only cell phones, but this phone gathered dust because no one used it anymore. As he placed the handset back in place, he saw the display showed five missed calls and a message from a number with a 360 area code, all from the day before. It wasn't Rod's number; his cell phone was still a 509 area code.

"Mom," Travis yelled as he stood back up. "Mom!"

The clatter of dishes stopped, and his mom appeared in the doorway drying her hands with a dish towel. "Travis, I've asked you a million times not to yell. What is it?"

He pointed at the phone, his hand shaking. "Did someone call for me recently?" The call could have been for his parents, he supposed, but as far as he knew they had no friends or connections in the northwest corner of Washington.

"Oh," Lenore gave the phone a withering glance as if the phone was at fault, "right, someone did call. I think his name was Cameron or something."

"What did he want? Why didn't you tell me?" The only Cameron Travis knew lived in Skagit and worked at the Loft.

His mother wrinkled her nose. "It slipped my mind."

"*What?*" Travis patted himself down looking for the keys to his truck. Cam wouldn't have called him here if there wasn't some sort of emergency; they weren't that close of friends. In fact, Travis didn't recall ever giving Cam his number. He'd left his keys in his jacket pocket after picking his truck up on the way back from the talk with his dad. Something terrible had happened. It was Rod, he knew it. Goose bumps formed on Travis's arms; beneath the long sleeves of his T-shirt, he had chills. He took a deep breath to calm himself.

Lenore actually looked angry. "It slipped my mind," she

repeated. "And see, what are you going to do now? Run off to Skagit to visit with Rod Beton? Leave your fiancée wondering where you've gone? I've always suspected he had his eye on you, and now you are running right to him. I should have put a stop to this a long time ago. I should have kept him out of the house when he admitted he was a gay." Her voice was shrill and still managed to drip with venom.

Out of the corner of his eye, Travis saw his dad stiffen. Shock, maybe? Michael started to push himself out of his chair. Travis put a palm out to forestall him from interfering. It really was now or never.

"Here's the thing, Mom. Lisa and I? We aren't getting married. I broke it off with her before she left. If I'm a lucky man, luckier than I deserve, someday I'll be marrying Rod. " Travis's cell phone caught on a thread as he jerked it from his back pocket, the string snapping as he dragged it out. With a shaking finger, he was able to jab Cam's number into his cell. It began to ring on the other end, and he watched his mom's eyes narrow further in anger. She stepped closer—what, was she going to try to grab his phone? Travis moved out of her reach, turning his back on her, while he waited for someone to pick up on the other end.

"Travis Michael Walker, if you think I am going to let you ruin this family with that... *homosexual*," she spat the word out, bitter and spiteful, "think again."

His dad intervened with a sharp "Lenore," as she stomped out of the room. His dad followed her, saying something else, but Travis didn't hear over the rushing in his ears.

A voice he hadn't heard in months came on the other end of the line. "Hello?"

"Cameron, it's Travis Walker." He shoved aside the terrible words his mother had said so he could focus. Rod needed him.

"Travis, where have you been? You are one hard man to get ahold of." Cam's voice, normally cheerful, was laced with worry and stress.

"What happened? Is Rod okay?" To his own ears, Travis's voice was shaky and thin. He could hear his own fear.

## 9

Rod thought maybe after the weird experience at the Loft Theo wouldn't message him again. Did he want to see Theo again? He wasn't sure, but in the spirit of creating a new life he figured he'd let whatever happened happen, and Theo was a funny guy. Regardless, Rod was mildly surprised when he got a text from Theo a few days later.

THEO: U WANT TO GO4A HIKE?

It was March, not exactly hiking season yet, but the day was pleasant enough—remarkable for March, actually. The sun peeked out occasionally as a southeast wind blew puffy clouds across the sky. He and Theo agreed to meet at a trailhead east of town. The trail ran along the Skagit River before heading up into the foothills of the North Cascades and promised views if they made it all the way up to the lookout.

It was good to get out of his apartment, Rod thought as he parked his truck off to the side. He'd been depressed; even video games were no fun. Theo wasn't there yet. Rod stood at the edge of the embankment and watched the river water swirl angrily below with the early spring runoff.

Gravel popped behind him. Turning, he saw a late-model small SUV pull in and stop next to his truck. The door swung open, and Theo emerged with a wave and a cheerful, "Hey!"

Rod spent so much time in the woods during the summer fighting fires that being in a non-charred forest was something close to novel. The deciduous maples and birches were just starting to leaf. Wildflowers weren't out yet, but the hike was still beautiful. As they made their way up the narrow trail, Rod let Theo do the talking while the green quiet of the forest seeped into his skin, smoothing him out.

About two miles in, they reached the first view point. It was a good thing they'd both dressed warmly; there was plenty of snow still sticking around at this elevation. The view looked westward toward the Skagit Valley, where Rod could see the signs of the coming spring everywhere. Fields were tilled and planted with the local crops. On one field Rod saw a flock of snow geese, white dots from where he and Theo stood, start to take off. He loved watching them lift off en masse and sort themselves into the V formation.

"So, who is he?" Theo's voice startled him.

"Who is who?"

"Who is the guy you're all tied up over? Is he worth it?"

Rod sighed, turning to look at his friend. "That obvious?"

"Yeah. Maybe it's because I've been there too." Theo gave him a sheepish smile. "I moved to Skagit to start again. I just couldn't be in Denver anymore... Anyway, who is he?"

Rod grinned ruefully at Theo before turning to look back over the valley. "We grew up together. I've known Travis since the third grade when I was the new kid in town and he was making sure I got fruit snacks when Mrs. Cathy handed them out. He also gave me one of his Pokémon cards."

The Betons had moved to Walla Walla when Rod was eight

and a half. He still remembered how scared he'd been that first day at school. Both of his parents had started new jobs. There'd been a quick visit to the playground over the weekend, but when Monday arrived, his mom walked him to the school bus, patted him on the shoulder, and told him to have a good day.

Luckily, he knew his teacher's name, and an older student from the bus helped him find the classroom once they arrived at school. Still, he panicked in the doorway while all the other kids rushed inside, parting around him like he was a rock in a human river until everyone was seated and he was left standing alone.

A kid with bright blond hair and a cowlick in his bangs that made him look a little mischievous saw him waiting there and yelled over, "Sit here!" patting the desk behind him.

"I'm so stupid." Rod shook his head. "I hung around waiting for him, waiting for the right time, and bam, out of the blue, he announces he's engaged to the girl next door."

"Ugh, that's awful. Not gay, then?"

"He's bi. He really is; I've seen him with both men and women pretty consistently over the years. So it's not a sexuality thing. It's a me thing."

Theo winced and frowned.

"Right? I'm just thankful I never said anything. I was trying to get up the courage when he announced the engagement." He blew out a long breath. "Less about me, more about you."

"I don't really want to talk about it... but, that night at the Loft, those jerks brought back some memories I'd rather forget."

Rod hoped he never saw those two guys again, especially if he was driving his truck.

"Travis..." Rod didn't want Theo to think Trav was a bad guy. "He didn't do anything wrong. I should have said something sooner, maybe. I don't know. I spent years being terrified that if I said anything it would ruin our friendship, and now it seems like our friendship is ruined anyway. I keep telling myself this is the way things are meant to be, but it sure doesn't feel like it."

"Maybe something will happen and he'll figure it out."

Rod snorted. "Travis is a lot of things: funny, brave, super smart—he graduated at the top of his class in college—did I mention sexy? He'd be a way better model for that calendar you were talking about. But he is not going to wake up and suddenly realize we are the next gay power couple."

"ANOTHER HIKE SOMETIME?" Theo asked as they scrambled down the trail toward their cars.

"Sounds great." Yeah, he and Theo were never going to be a thing, but if he'd managed to make a new friend, maybe this move to Skagit would turn out to have been a good choice.

Theo sketched a quick wave before pulling out onto the highway toward town. Rod watched as his taillights disappeared around the curve, and then he followed. The truck's radio was tuned to an alternative station and the signal wasn't great, dropping in and out as Rod managed the curves and dips of the road.

Even though it wasn't quite spring, there were a few early-bird RVers on the road. Would he ever be that person? Old, happily married, or at least with a partner. He imagined himself and Travis (no matter how hard he tried, Travis's handsome face always ended up on his imaginary future partner) manhandling one of those behemoths down a long highway, amiably arguing about which one of them had taken the wrong turn and where they were going to stop for the night. It was a nice dream, anyway.

Maybe Rod was tired, maybe he wasn't paying attention to the road, maybe it wasn't his fault at all. Rod would never know; his memory of the accident was never clear. One minute he was driving, thinking about life, enjoying the unusual March sunshine; the next there was a cacophony of sound, screeching, a frantic horn, metal shearing. Then a resolute silence. At one point the silence was broken by sirens, lights, and rhythmic beeping, but soon even that faded from Rod's consciousness.

The silence was soothing. He liked the quiet, it made him feel safe. It was good for him to rest; it seemed he'd been working too hard. Maybe he should take time off more often. There was another thought hovering in the background, waiting for him to acknowledge it, but he was too tired to decipher it.

There was no white light, so Rod didn't think he was dead, and there seemed to be a lot of chatter, but he didn't open his eyes to see who was there. It seemed to him if he was in the afterlife it would be quieter. There was no single voice he recognized; they all blurred together, unintelligible low murmurs, a hum. There were other sounds too, but Rod focused on the voices. He liked the sound of them, the way they rose and fell with a predictable soothing cadence.

Once, as a young child, he'd been sick—the flu, maybe—and his parents took turns reading aloud to him. He didn't think they were the ones reading now (although someone *was* reading, Rod knew it). His parents divorced when he left for college, and he hadn't seen much of either of them since. His mom had moved to Ohio. Why would Rod want to visit Ohio? His dad had remarried and now lived in Boise with his new family. Rod often wondered why they'd bothered staying married so long if they were just going to bugger off as soon as he was out of the house.

Well, there was the gay thing too. His dad had listened without interrupting when Rod came out to him and then said he hoped Rod understood that while *he* had no problem with the gay lifestyle... blah blah blah. His mom had said she loved him and then moved to Ohio. That's why he'd spent so much time with Travis even though Lenore Walker had warned him off. Travis was his only family.

Except Travis was getting married. To Lisa Harris.

Rod's eyes flew open. Well, it seemed like they flew open; in reality his eyes creaked apart at most a quarter of an inch. His eyelids were heavy as lead, and his lashes were stuck together.

The lights in the room were turned down, or maybe it was nighttime. Through his tangled lashes, Rod recognized Travis's disheveled form slumped in a chair next to the bed with a book open but facedown in his lap. He was hunched, trying to fit his big body into the chair; his head was at an angle that couldn't be comfortable.

Where was he, and what was Travis doing here? Rod let his gaze drift across Travis's profile, his strong straight nose, his messy blond hair.

He must have made some sort of sound he was unaware of. Travis's head shot up, his eyes wide. "You're awake. I'll get the nurse."

That answered the question of where Rod was. Travis rushed out of the room before Rod could articulate a reply. The nurse summoned, Travis returned to hover next to the bed, shifting his weight from one foot to the other but not saying anything.

Travis was rarely quiet. Rod wanted to reach out a hand to reassure him, but his left arm was immobilized. In fact, he was covered with all sorts of tubes and wires. And he ached.

A dark-haired woman about his age wearing light blue scrubs swept into the room.

"Mr. Beton, nice to see you awake. You gave us a bit of a scare. How are you feeling?"

"Like I was hit by a truck," Rod rasped. His throat was raw, and it hurt to talk.

"You *were* hit by a fucking truck, you asshole," Travis barked out.

The nurse, her name tag emblazoned with the name

Melinda, shot Travis a quelling look. Travis didn't look particularly quelled; he looked mad and scared with a hint of relief.

"You were in an accident, Mr. Beton. In a few minutes the doctor will be here, and she will run you through a few tests. In the meantime I'll get you a cup of ice."

The doctor came in a few minutes later, and by that time Rod was ready to go back to sleep. The doctor insisted on shining a light in his eyes, poking and prodding, asking him questions about breathing, pain level, etc. Rod tried to answer, but he was tired and wanted to escape back into the cocoon of sleep.

"He just woke up, you think you can go a little easy on him?" There was a frown in Travis's voice.

Rod let his eyes shut all the way. Keeping them open any longer wasn't an option.

"Mr. Walker—" There was a hint of impatience to the doctor's tone. Rod smirked. Travis hated being called Mr. Walker. "—this is my job. I'm very good at it. Please let me finish without interruption."

"Is Rod going to be okay?" There it was, the undertone of worry Rod had detected.

"Now that he's awake, all signs indicate he will recover fully. It's not going to be easy; there will be mobility issues until the bone and tissue in his leg heal, and a punctured lung is something to be very careful with. It's going to take time, and he is going to need help at home."

"When can he go home?"

"That is up to Mr. Beton's body. I'd like him to be a little more alert. Physical therapy will start tomorrow. The punctured lung is healing nicely, but it's six to eight weeks before he'll be safe to go for a jog. Of course his leg needs to heal as well, so his full recovery will be longer than that."

Rod let himself fall back into sleep. Travis would take care of everything.

THE NEXT TIME Rod woke up, Travis was gone and Cameron was in his place.

"Where's Travis?" Rod asked, his voice hoarse.

Cameron looked up from what he was doing on his phone, smiling at him. "Hey, there you are. The doc said you were only sleeping now, but still... How are you feeling? Travis went to take care of a few things. Should I get the nurse?"

"Water sounds good." He did a mental assessment of how he felt. Thirsty, stiff, achy; his left leg and arm seemed hot, but the rest of his body felt okay. "I guess I feel all right for being in an accident. What happened?"

The smile slipped off his friend's face. "You never told me you put me down as your emergency contact. Getting that phone call from the hospital..."

Rod had written Cameron down on his employment paperwork because he was irritated with Travis and both his parents were too far away. Something he'd forgotten until this moment. "How'd they get your number?" As far as Rod knew, it was only on the paperwork he'd filled out for the bus company.

"Responders found some stuff in your truck, I think, with the name of the place you work for. They're the ones who called me. Jeez, Rod, everybody's been scared."

"My truck?"

"Bless that 1980s steel beast. It saved your life. Mangled you a bit, but saved your life. You're gonna need a new truck. The guy that hit you was driving too fast pulling a trailer. He overcorrected and ended up pushing you into a wall of rock."

Rod contemplated that his truck was gone. He loved that truck. The first time he'd kissed a boy it had been in the cab of that truck. Of course Chad Owens never spoke to him again after that... so maybe the truck wasn't full of such good memories.

"So, how'd Travis find out?"

"I called him. Well, I called his house in Walla Walla. Left a message with someone who I think is his mother. To be honest, I wasn't sure she was going to tell him. But he showed up and has been here ever since."

"How long was I out?"

"Four days. The docs kept telling us you would wake up when you were ready, your brain was active... but dude... really? Don't do that again." Cam shook his head.

"Travis has been here the whole time?" There was no way that was going over well with his family.

"About that. Rod, the guy is a serious hot mess. I had no idea. You two need to figure your shit out. He keeps leaving to take calls from his family or something."

"And you wonder why I stayed in a coma for four days," Rod muttered.

"Don't joke about that, asshole. What are you going to do about Travis?"

"Go back to sleep?"

Cam shot him a glare.

"What am I supposed to do, Cam? He's getting married, his mother hates me, his dad's indifferent. I have no idea about his kid sister. I'm moving on. I should have years ago."

"I still think you should tell him how you feel."

"One, it's too late: he's getting married. Two, I did. Kind of. I left a note." Thankfully Travis had never mentioned it, so Rod could pretend he'd never left it for him to find.

The nurse bustled in just then, which Rod was thankful for. By the time she was done checking everything and asking personal questions, the moment for more conversation about

Travis had passed. The man himself showed back up as the nurse was leaving, and Cameron left too, with the promise he'd be back to visit, but he had a bunch of shifts coming up.

"Unless they let you out. Be sure to keep us updated." With that, Cameron left Rod and Travis alone.

Travis shoved his cell phone into his pocket, wearing a slightly hunted expression.

"How's Lisa?" Rod asked wearily. He didn't dislike Lisa; they'd never spent enough time together for him to like or dislike her. She'd hung around with their crowd of friends, but Lisa was a 4-H horsey girl, always raising goats or rabbits or something, riding in the Fourth of July parade. Rod and Travis rode dirt bikes and went hiking when Travis wasn't being fielded for some sports team. But she and Travis had been neighbors all their lives. And now, apparently, lovers.

Travis was good at organized sports, always one of the best at hitting, catching fly balls, making three-pointers from the middle of the basketball court... but he didn't enjoy it. Something his folks didn't seem to understand. Rod also remembered Travis's sister was just as good at all that, but they didn't make nearly the big deal of her that they did Travis.

"I don't want to talk about Lisa right now. She's fine." He started to sit down on the chair next to Rod's bed but changed his mind mid-sit, perching instead on the edge of the bed. "You scared the crap out of me. They had to use the Jaws of Life to extract you from your truck. If you'd been driving anything else, you'd be dead." Travis's voice sounded funny.

Rod rolled his head on the pillow to look at his friend, cataloging his general appearance. Travis looked terrible. Rod probably looked terrible too, but he had an excuse. Travis normally looked like a rugged, slightly hipster mountain man. Scruffy, but with a spark of life that had proved impossible for Rod to deny.

Today he was pale and careworn, as if he hadn't been sleeping well.

Rod did his best to refocus, but he was sleepy again. Travis was still speaking. "You almost died. And if Cameron hadn't figured out how to find me, I wouldn't have known. I came as soon as I heard. Don't ever do that to me again." Rod shut his eyes as Travis talked, letting himself fantasize that Travis had come because he cared for Rod as more than just his best buddy.

On Monday morning the physical therapist departed (no doubt fleeing Rod's bad humor), declaring Rod would soon be able to go home—contingent upon the doctor signing off—as long as he continued his exercises, continued PT for time immemorial, and promised to put no weight on his left leg until they okayed it in triplicate: at least sixteen weeks. Rod wanted out of the hospital badly enough to promise, even though the exercises made his eyes tear up and he wanted to beg for a painkiller when they were finished.

The cheery therapist reminded him daily he was lucky to have his leg with a good possibility of regaining full use of it, as it had nearly been crushed in the accident. Rod knew that. But when she was manipulating it back and forth, sideways, seemingly backward—all for the sake of mobility—teaching him to use crutches properly and being all freaking happy, he didn't feel grateful.

He was in an especially foul humor because he'd had a vivid dream about Travis. It was more memory than dream; he must have fallen asleep thinking about their childhood or something. The dream/memory was from the summer when they were both fourteen. It had been especially hot that year. The haze of wheat dust hung heavily in the sky, creating intense sunsets but making farmers and townies alike worry about fire danger.

The bike ride from Rod's house to Travis's was long, and it was already hot that morning. On a typical day, it would creep over a hundred degrees by three p.m. By the time Rod arrived at the Walker place out in the valley, it was in the eighties and he was drenched with sweat and covered by road dust from all the trucks passing him. One direction they were full of freshly harvested wheat heading for the closest silo, the other they were empty and ready for another load. Travis met him at the front of the house, not even waiting for Rod to prop his bike against the side.

"Come on! I'm gonna show you something today!"

Rod's parents were out of town; where, he now couldn't remember. He had refused to go. Summer was sacred time when he and Trav hung out as much as they could. Travis was supposed to be working for his dad. When Michael had realized that Rod had nowhere to be and was going to be underfoot regardless, he laughingly hired him to keep Travis out of trouble.

"You know the routine, son: help Travis think before he acts. I'll pay you ten bucks a day."

In the dream they went from standing by Rod's bike to the cab of a pickup truck. In reality it had taken Travis a lot of fast-talking to get Rod to take the keys, but Rod had wanted to learn to drive, and his self-preservation instinct was drowned out by the intense desire to get behind the wheel of the big pickup truck.

"Everybody needs to know how to drive, Rod! My dad said so."

"I don't think he meant me."

"It's totally legal, on a farm you don't have to be sixteen to drive."

Rod was certain Travis was glossing over some important legal points, but sitting behind the wheel of the farm truck was intoxicating. It didn't matter that it was a beat-up truck, over thirty years old and closing in on three hundred thousand miles; to Rod it was a glorious freedom. A sign of adulthood.

To give Trav credit, both of them actually, ninety percent of the driving lesson went really well. Rod *had* practiced a little with his own dad in their boring sedan, but that was nothing like being behind the wheel of the farm truck, so much higher off the ground with a much more powerful engine.

Michael was having them take water and lunch out to the various crews across the Walker spread. Rod was driving the truck upward along a track that zigzagged up one of the rolling hills of the Palouse where wheat was being harvested that day, when he glanced over at Travis for just a second.

It was the longest second of his life. It had been fourteen years since that moment, and Rod could still recall with intense clarity Travis's silhouette as he stared out the windshield, watching where Rod was driving. The track was narrow and steep, and thick dust billowed out behind them as Rod kept the truck slowly moving up the hillside. At the time it seemed like he could see into the future and know what Travis was going to look like as a grown man.

"You're riding the clutch. You gotta go faster or you're gonna stall out," Travis said matter-of-factly.

The truck stalled. Rod panicked, forgetting to stomp on the brake, instead hitting the gas and flooding the engine. The odor of gasoline permeated the cab. It freaked him out, and all he could think was that, between the gasoline and the wheat dust, there was going to be a fire. Everyone worried about fire out there, and every year there were a few fires caused by careless-ness or lightning.

Rod was so scared he couldn't even speak. On either side of

the truck, the hillside fell down and away. They were perched at the top of a golden wave of wheat; all he could see was the undulating landscape in every direction, the horizon occasionally marred by farm buildings or irrigation turbines. There was nowhere to pull aside.

"It's okay, stomp on the emergency brake," Travis instructed.

Rod scrambled, looking for the brake. He had no idea where it was; in his parents' cars it was always between the front seats.

"It's to your left, on the floor." Travis's voice was steady.

The truck started moving backward, and Rod couldn't get his hands off the steering wheel. Next thing he knew, Travis was climbing over him, jamming himself between Rod and the steering wheel, forcing him to let go. Travis was sitting in Rod's lap with his ass pressing against Rod. Trav stomped on the foot brake before twisting around to the left and setting the emergency brake, which was conveniently located to the far left of Rod's feet.

By then, Rod already knew he didn't like girls the way most of his other friends did. He didn't dislike them, but he sure didn't want to kiss any of them, and the porno stuff that Mitchell Atkins had brought and shared around under the bleachers was unsettling. To suddenly have an erection during a near-death experience was shocking and embarrassing. As quickly as he could, he scrambled out from under Travis's ass.

"Dad says to wait a few minutes for the carburetor to drain and then try restarting. So, hey, guess what?"

Rod arranged himself on the other side of the truck's bench seat, trying to hide his erection and not freak out about nearly running them off the road.

"What?"

"Me and Shauna White kissed last night."

Rod woke up.

.   .   .

REALLY? That what his subconscious wanted to remind him of? Rod petulantly snatched the remote for the TV, turning the thing on even though all that was showing right now was reruns on ESPN and Mexican soap operas. He couldn't stomach the news these days.

He was watching a telenovela through half-open eyelids, pretending he was practicing his Spanish and very interested in the over-the-top dramatic plotline, not brooding about the dream he'd had, when a voice cut across his thoughts.

"You're awake!"

Travis wore a huge grin as he practically bounced into Rod's room, a lot like Tigger. Rod felt like Eeyore. *Somebody* certainly was in a good mood. Trav plopped himself down on the edge of Rod's bed, causing it to dip. Since Rod first woke up in the hospital, Travis had made a habit of sitting next to him on the bed instead of using the chair.

"There's a perfectly good chair, you know."

"Aw, is somebody in a bad mood?" Travis teased.

Rod felt himself crack a smile involuntarily. God fucking dammit, it was impossible for him to be out of sorts around Travis. He hated that he responded like that.

"Guess what, though. I have grrrreaat news!" Maybe Tony the Tiger instead of Tigger.

"What?" Rod knew he sounded surly and ungrateful. But dammit, he was emotionally compromised and messed up in the head, and he'd just had that dream, and he wanted to know why Travis was here. And when he was leaving. Rod knew he needed to prepare himself, but he wasn't ready for that yet. He wanted something he couldn't have, and it seemed that even being in a terrible car accident hadn't knocked any sense into him.

"I rented us a place." Travis was grinning like a fool now. He had a great smile, not like Rod, who ended up looking like he needed to go to the bathroom when he smiled hard.

"What the fuck?" Rod had a place, thank you very much. "I have a place."

"Yeah, but it's upstairs in an old building, and I found a great house! It guess it's a bungalow. It's small but has two bedrooms. Cam helped me find it. And I tracked down your landlord and he's being pretty cool; I'm paying rent through the end of April, but he's letting you out of the lease."

Rod gaped at his friend. What the hell?

Rod did not know what to think. Did. Not. Know. What. To. Think. Travis watched him, clearly waiting for some sort of response.

"Cam helped you?" Rod managed to squeak out.

"Yeah. Some college guys are moving out today, and I'm moving your stuff over tomorrow. That way, when you get out, you'll have a place."

"What?" Rod sputtered. "How is this happening? How can you be doing all of this? I can't afford a house by myself. This is ridiculous."

Travis laughed. "It's not ridiculous, it's the only thing that makes any sense at all. You're going to need help doing your exercises and getting back and forth to doctors' appointments—hell, you're going to need help getting your ass to the bathroom for a while. The physical therapist told me if you didn't have someone to help at home, you'd need to go to an assisted care facility until you were mobile. Believe me, this is the best solution."

"But..." Rod couldn't think of anything to say. Travis staying? He'd fantasized about him and Travis being together, Travis moving to Skagit—after that the details were foggy, because Travis moving to Skagit would never happen—but... "What about the farm?"

Travis waved off his protest, but Rod caught that Travis didn't exactly look him in the eye, instead focusing somewhere just above his shoulder. "I've got everything taken care of. Don't worry about a thing."

Rod narrowed his gaze at Travis, who was still inspecting the wall behind Rod. Memories surfaced of several situations over the years that Rod most certainly should have worried about when Travis had that look on his face.

He didn't get the chance to interrogate him, though; one of the day nurses poked her head through the open door.

"Mr. Beton? Are you feeling up to several guests? There are some folks out here who are anxious to see you."

There was muffled whispering and shuffling coming from the hallway, followed by hushing and shushing noises. Rod couldn't imagine who was out there. His few friends in Skagit had already been by to visit. He nodded his okay. The nurse motioned to someone, and a few seconds later a humongous balloon bouquet floated into the room. It took Rod a second to realize there were several pairs of short legs underneath the balloons, which were large enough to obscure whoever was holding them.

Rod had held it together when the doctor told him his leg was touch-and-go at first; he'd managed not to cry when the physical therapist performed torture on him; he'd stoically accepted that even if either of his parents knew about the accident, they wouldn't make the trip to see for themselves that he was going to recover. So why, when three grubby second- and third-graders from the school bus route showed up in his room with balloons, did he start to cry?

Travis stood up so the kids could come closer to the bed.

"Mr. Beton, we brought you balloons." Maurice spoke for the group; not surprising, since he was also one of the most vocal kids riding the bus route. "Are you going to be okay now?

Everyone on the bus is very worried about you. Me and Vincent and Sydney are the only ones who could come, because there are only three back seats in the car. My mom brought us." Maurice tagged that last part on the end as if he was worried Rod would think they'd driven themselves.

Rod wiped his eyes of the offending moisture, offering as cheery a grin as possible to his bus kids. Maurice approached the bed cautiously. He was a cute kid, taller than the rest, with curly dark hair. There was a gap between his front teeth where he'd lost a baby tooth since Rod had last seen him.

"Mom said there was an accident and you broke your leg."

"Mom" came toward the bed. Rod had seen her before, waiting at Maurice's stop.

"Hi, I hope this is okay. Maurice has been relentless about visiting. I'm Shanda, by the way."

"Rod, the bus driver, and," he motioned toward Travis, "this is my friend Travis."

Travis used his thousand-watt smile on Shanda, stepping forward to shake her hand.

"Travis is the one I fight fires with in the summer." Although he wouldn't be doing much of that soon, or maybe ever again. Rod's comment seemed to break the ice for the kids, and they swarmed closer to the bed, full of questions, wanting to know what had happened, did he have a bionic leg now, could they see it? Was it cool fighting fires? Did they get to wear the same kind of fire gear as regular firefighters? Rod had forgotten how inquisitive they all were.

When would he be driving the school bus again, they asked. The substitute driver was not nearly as cool and fun. Were they going to be able to finish the story they had started, because they had ideas about what should happen next.

Travis hung back from the group, watching as the kids peppered Rod with questions. Eventually Sydney, the quietest of the three, pointed at him and whispered, "You're Mr. Beton's friend?"

Sydney's question seemed to snap Travis from some sort of reverie; he shook his head and brought his focus back to the room. Rod wondered what he'd been thinking about.

Travis stuck out his hand for Sydney to shake. "Yep, Travis Walker. I've known Rod a long time, since I was your age. What's your name?"

Sydney eyed him with suspicion. "*Mr. Beton* is our school bus driver." Rod chuckled at Sydney's rebuke of Travis's familiarity.

Travis nodded, crouching so he and Sydney were eye to eye. "Is he a good bus driver?"

"Yes, he always waits for kids if they're late. And he helps us write stories. My name is Sydney." Sydney had a slight lisp that made his s's breathy. Apparently satisfied with Travis, Sydney joined back in the conversation Maurice and Vincent were having about the fate of the space-adventuring amphibians Rod and the bus riders were "writing."

Shanda stood at the back of the room watching the kids interact with Rod, all of them careful of his leg and steering clear of the end of the bed. Someone, probably the nurse, had warned them about his injuries, so while they asked a few questions, they didn't focus on them except to ask if he was going to be okay. He was glad the worst of the bruising had faded. They stayed until Maurice started to get antsy.

Shanda took her son by the hand, had the kids say goodbye, and led everyone out of the room. They tried to linger, but eventually they all followed Shanda out and down the hallway. Rod could hear them chattering and Shanda offering ice cream on the way home. The room was empty without them.

Somewhere around the middle of the kids' visit Travis had snuck out, avoiding the conversation that Rod was determined to have with him. But the interaction had tired him more than he expected, and with the room finally empty he found his eyes drifting shut with the TV still playing in the background. He'd have the conversation with Travis in due time; he wouldn't be able to avoid it for long. A last thought flitted through his mind before he fell asleep: where was Jasper? If an offer to visit Mr. Beton had been made, he knew Jasper would have come if he could.

## 10

Travis had reserved the closest hotel room to the hospital he could find. It was boring, but it had the necessities: a bed, and a TV for white noise when he slept. He hadn't been entirely truthful with Rod when he'd claimed he had everything under control, and the evidence of the wobble in his plans was unmistakable as his phone continued to blow up.

Lenore's messages had filled up his voice mail. Travis finally stopped deleting them so she couldn't leave any more, because he was tired of hearing her rant at him. Her voice was full of rage and hate and vitriol he'd never imagined she harbored. The messages were all the same, berating Travis for leaving Walla Walla, for still being gone, for his friendship with Rod, for disappointing her, for... well, it sure seemed like there wasn't much about Travis's life Lenore *didn't* have an opinion about.

He talked to his dad every day through Skype. His dad was terrible with computer stuff, but Abigail had taught him how to video chat. Michael wanted updates on Rod, and Travis needed to stay updated on what was happening with the spring planting. He hadn't told Michael about the messages Lenore was leaving, and it turned out he didn't have to.

Travis felt terrible—like a traitor—for not being home this time of year. It was the time when they would be able to assess how well the wheat did over the winter and they'd be getting ready to sow, but he couldn't leave Skagit now. He knew if he left, the slim chance he had at fixing things between him and Rod would vanish.

Wrong time to run away from home. Although home, it seemed, wasn't as set in stone as he'd thought.

Travis was in the elevator when his phone buzzed; luckily it was his dad's number.

"Dad, I'm sorry," Travis began. It seemed like he started every conversation these days with an apology.

His dad interrupted him. "I said don't worry about it, son, and I meant it. You do what you need to do. I'll take care of things here. We have a good staff."

They did have a good staff, but it was still wrong of him not to be there helping out. The elevator doors slid open and Travis stepped out, slowly making his way down the long hallway to his room.

Michael cleared his throat. "I'm sorry for what Lenore has put you through. I found her phone last night; that text was wrong."

Travis wanted to ask which one. The sheer number of increasingly horrible texts from his mother was hard to get his head around. "Dad—"

Michael took a breath and continued speaking before Travis could think of anything to say. "Church has always bored me, but I've read the Gospels, and nowhere does it say anything about gay people being sinners or wrong. What's wrong is being so full of hate that it spills over onto other people. Into your family. You are my son, and I love you unconditionally, same as I love your sister. Try not to worry about your mother." Another deep breath. "We're having some hard conversations. Just know that I support you and whatever you choose."

Travis stared at the door, room number 235. He shook his head, reaching into his back pocket for the room key. His dad had just told him everything would be all right, and Travis believed him.

"I love you too, Dad." Words Travis probably hadn't said since he was eight. Far too long.

Travis slid the key card across the reader and the door lights blinked green. As he pushed the door open, he considered that for all the wild childhood escapades he'd gotten up to—mostly with Rod—he'd never been on the receiving end of his mom's vitriol before. That had always been Abigail.

He'd been tempted but decided against blocking his mom's phone number. He'd been holding on to a scrap of hope that she would stop, come to her senses, but that hope was fading. It was just about time for another call. Blocking her felt like cheating; he had disappointed her, and he deserved her anger. It seemed better to give her an outlet than to ignore the situation.

He tossed his keys on the counter next to the tiny coffeepot and collapsed onto the too-soft mattress. The maid had been in earlier, so the room was tidy and the bed made, not that Travis had been spending much time there. Yesterday he'd signed the lease for the house Cameron had helped him find. He couldn't wait; he wanted Rod out of the hospital and home so they could start moving forward. So Travis could see if he would be able to make things right.

God, he needed to talk to Abigail. But what he really wanted to do was crawl under the covers and pull them over his head for a while. Until he managed to straighten his life out. He was walking a razor's edge between happiness, because he could almost see the future he imagined for Rod and himself, and despair, because he still had so many things to sort out. Not the least of which was what he was going to do in Skagit. Or about his mother.

His phone vibrated. He glanced at it, the words not fully making sense in the truncated preview screen, but he got the gist.

"Fucking fuck," he muttered to the empty room.


AFTER READING the text from his mother, Travis shut his eyes. He had no idea what it meant. He didn't think his dad would tell her where he was staying or give out any information about Rod. Travis was worried about Michael; his parents may not have had an overtly happy relationship, but he didn't think his dad had been *un*happy. Now? Travis didn't know. Just another thing to feel guilty about.

He didn't intend to fall asleep; it was only late afternoon, but somehow he found himself slipping into memories of him and Rod some time in high school.

They been up to no good, as usual, and—as usual—it was Travis's idea. Rod was along not because he thought the plan was great but because he "figured somebody needed to be around to call 911." Travis recalled with clarity the sarcasm dripping from Rod's voice.

There was nothing like most of a fifth of Travis's friend Jack D. for coming up with great ideas.

"We can't go to the ocean, so we'll bring the ocean to us!"

It was mid-August. Harvest was mostly over, and everyone was tired of the incessant heat. The crew they hung out with had already hit every possible legal thing to do in a small town over the summer, and plenty of illegal ones too. They'd even checked out the water park in the next town over, but it was only a swimming pool on steroids. Travis was hot, and damn, he wanted to see the ocean.

"Trav, I don't know." Rod hadn't hit his growth spurt yet; at sixteen he was just hitting five foot five and scrawny. Most of them were still on the small side. Not Travis, though. He'd shot up four inches since January, and he'd been throwing hay around all summer, packing on more muscle.

"What could go wrong?" Somewhere in the back of his head a little voice was reciting a long list of things that could go wrong, but he was choosing to ignore it. The buzz of grasshoppers and clicks of other bugs in the tall grass along the parking lot where they were hanging out finishing that bottle of Jack were like a chant egging Travis on.

He wanted to see the ocean, but his parents never wanted to go anywhere fun. Family vacations were always back to Missouri or some other flat, boring state where all they did was chase fireflies and count bug bites. Last year Abigail had vomited in the car on the first day, making the trip a living nightmare. They were leaving for the hated family trip tomorrow, and Travis had threatened her within an inch of her life if something like that happened this year.

"I'll stand on the truck, and you'll drive real slow—"

"I am not driving. No way." Rod was shaking his head. His dark hair had grown out over the summer, and it was kind of curly, something Travis had never noticed before. He blinked, wondering where the thought had come from.

"Fine." Travis turned to Chad. "You drive. Slowly speed up while I stand on the cab."

He'd been bored out of his mind surfing the internet the week before when he'd found this gem. He'd been on his own because Rod's parents had dragged him off on some kind of weird family trip for almost two weeks. Weird because Rod's family never went anywhere.

Of course he'd *had* to watch a video showing this guy surfing on his car. Travis knew he could do it way better than the guy in the video—who'd fallen off and, man, did that look like it hurt. There were some nut jobs who did it at high speed on the freeway. Travis wasn't going to be going that fast, just enough to feel a breeze across his skin and pretend he was floating in the ocean.

When he opened his eyes, Rod was leaning over him, dark eyes full of fury battling with concern. Travis was having trouble pulling air into his lungs, and things were generally a bit fuzzy.

"What happened?" he wheezed. Fuck, that hurt. Almost as bad as when he'd been tackled during a game by the kid from Waitsburg who was built like a Mack truck.

"Chad hit the fucking gas pedal, and you slammed into the bed of the truck! God, you are such an asshole!"

"Why am I the asshole?" All Travis knew was that he could hardly breathe and the back of his head throbbed from where he'd hit the bed of the pickup. Sitting up, he put a hand to the back of his head. He could feel a bump but no blood.

Rod crouched over him, the late afternoon sunshine a halo behind his head. "What day is it?"

"What?"

"What fucking day is it?" Rod's expression was grim. Travis would have laughed if he had any air left in his lungs.

"Jeez, it's Thursday. My name is Travis Walker. I've seen this movie, Nurse Nancy."

Rod punched him in the arm before hopping out of the back of the truck and stomping over to the edge of the grass.

All the other guys had vanished, except for Chad, who looked edgy as heck. "Are you all right, man? I think I gotta get going."

Travis crawled out of the truck, landing on his ass in the dirt. Chad didn't even ask if Travis needed a ride. Chad gunned the engine, then raced off, a cloud of dust billowing in his wake. Travis half expected Rod to leave too. He didn't. He was mad as hell, but he drove Travis home and even stayed up with him to make sure he didn't fall asleep and not wake up, because Rod had seen that movie too.

When Travis woke up forty-five minutes later, he was groggy and disoriented. And he still had no idea how to stop his mother from coming to Skagit to "talk some sense into" him.

## 11

T he next morning, even though he'd awakened to the news he was officially cleared to go home, Rod was in a foul humor. He didn't even want to be around himself. He'd spent all night thinking about what Travis had said about renting a house and fantasizing about what their lives together would be like. Having Travis say those words made the fantasy more elaborate, which made Rod angry.

A house? Talking to his landlord? The hell. What the fucking hell? Rod couldn't afford an entire house on his own. Maybe a room in a house—or a tiny house like the kind featured on home improvement shows. Not a real house; that kind of expense would blow through his savings.

Unless Travis was planning on staying.

No, he couldn't think that.

Rod forced the thought into a deep, dark box in his head. That path led nowhere good. His stomach got all weird and fluttery, and not in a way he could blame on the medications he'd been forced to take, so he pushed the thought to the back of his mind where it belonged.

Travis couldn't stay in Skagit. He had his life all set for him in

Walla Walla. Landowner and wheat farmer, with more money than god. The golden boy, born with a silver spoon in his mouth. He'd never had to work for anything; it had all been handed to him. He'd grown up knowing he would never have to worry about where he lived or if he had a job. The Walker empire awaited him.

Rod knew he was being unfair, and that made him even more irritable. Travis didn't care that he'd come from more money than Rod. He never brought it up at all. Even in college when it could have really been a big deal, Travis never did anything that Rod couldn't afford.

Maybe it was Rod who had the problem.

Shit. He shut his eyes for a second, letting the thought settle in his brain.

He'd never thought about that before, not really. Was he envious of Travis's money? It wasn't as if Travis flaunted it. Hell, when Rod had decided to try firefighting, Travis had signed his contract at the same time. He certainly didn't need the money, as his college education had been fully paid for.

God, he was a dick.

He scooted over to the side of the hospital bed and very carefully swung his legs over. There was a soft cast on his left leg, extending from the top of his thigh to his toes. He supposed he should count himself lucky that he wasn't encased in plaster, although maybe they didn't do that kind of thing these days. He didn't feel lucky right now; he felt like throwing something.

A knock on his door interrupted his bad temper. Rod called out for whoever it was to come in, and Cameron poked his head into the room, a big, irritating smile on his handsome face.

"You decent?"

"No, but modesty isn't something well-guarded in this place. I don't think there's a part of my body that hasn't been on public display at this point."

"Want some help getting dressed?" Cam sauntered in, shutting the door behind him.

Did he want help? No. Did he need it? Yes.

"That'd be great," he managed to grind out.

At some point someone had dropped off street clothes so Rod wouldn't have to leave St. Joe's in a hospital gown. He felt like an old man needing help to put on the loose cotton shorts, T-shirt, and zip-up hoodie, but finally he was dressed. The doctor had already signed his discharge papers, and Rod had listened carefully to the instructions from the physical therapist.

"Tell me about this house you helped Travis find," Rod demanded.

Cameron grinned again. "It's near downtown, about six blocks from the Booking Room. Another friend knew about it, so me and Trav got first dibs looking at it. It's pretty small, but two bedrooms, single bath, the kitchen was redone a few years ago, and it has a huge backyard. Oh, and a full basement."

"And why is Travis going to all this trouble?"

Cameron raised his eyebrows so high that they nearly disappeared into his hairline. "The two of you have got to be the most frustrating—"

Cameron didn't finish his sentence because, as if he had been summoned by the devil himself, Travis appeared in the doorway, a huge smile on his face too. Rod couldn't help but smile back. It was infuriating how his body and soul responded to this man.

"Ready to go?" Travis asked.

Both Travis and Cam were vibrating with excitement, and it was beyond Rod's pay grade to be a bastard when they were both so hyped up.

"Fine, let's do this thing."

Cameron walked next to the wheelchair while Travis pushed Rod toward the car. In the ten days Rod had been in the hospital, spring had officially arrived in Skagit. Being outside felt incredible, in spite of the clouds overhead and the steady mist. Mother Earth had been hinting around about spring when he and Theo were hiking before the accident.

Theo. Crap. He'd completely forgotten about Theo.

"Do you guys know what happened to my phone?" He figured it was gone, but...

"If it was in your truck, it's gone," Cameron said.

"Shit."

"What?" Travis and Cameron chimed together.

"Nothing." Rod was not going to bring up Theo right now. He'd figure out some way to get ahold of him.

They arrived at Travis's behemoth truck. Rod stared up at the thing. Somehow he'd forgotten how big it was. He was going to need help getting into the passenger seat. The initial joy at being out of the hospital dissipated as the reality of his recovery and general helplessness hit home.

"You couldn't have driven something more practical?" Never mind that when he got around to replacing his truck it would be just as big. The accident had been ruled the other driver's fault, and once the insurance companies finished bargaining, Rod would get a check toward a new truck. If he was lucky, it would be enough for a down payment.

"If I'd driven something more practical, you would have told me there was nothing wrong with you and asked why I changed rides."

It seemed Travis knew him pretty damn well.

ROD HAD to admit he liked the house—but only to himself. He'd be damned if he said anything out loud to encourage Travis any further. It pained him. He knew he would get attached to living in it, and in his head he would be playing house with Travis: his fantasy come to life. And at the end of the day Travis would go back home, leaving Rod to try to put his heart back together. Again.

A small voice in the back of his mind pointed out that Travis had rented the house. Travis had not gone back to Walla Walla. He had not mentioned Lisa or anything about a wedding. In fact, Travis had been studiously ignoring any references Rod made to the subject. What, exactly, was going on, Rod wondered.

Rod couldn't listen to that voice. He just couldn't.

"Check this out." Travis led Rod carefully across the small living room to the dining area, where a large window looked out on a backyard that appeared to be populated with fruit trees. What kind, Rod wasn't sure.

Spring had arrived in full force while he was in the hospital, and the trees were dense with pink and white blossoms. A breeze blew into the yard, and a multitude of petals drifted to the ground in a mini snowstorm.

"Beautiful." That was the only thing Rod could say, because it was. Absolutely beautiful. But his leg was starting to throb more insistently. "I should sit down."

"Of course, I'm sorry. I just wanted you to see that."

Travis helped him over to the couch, making sure his leg didn't bang into any of the boxes or furniture strewn across the communal space.

Rod stopped and stared at a couch that was definitely not the one he had bought secondhand a few months ago. This couch had a dark brown, soft-looking leather cover and was large enough for three big guys to sit comfortably, or two guys to lie on without their toes touching the armrests. He wanted to hate it. He didn't hate it.

"What happened to my couch? It was a perfectly good couch."

"I found a better couch."

"What was wrong with the couch I already had? I can't afford all this new stuff!" God dammit, now he was angry. Angry that he'd been in a car accident and stuck in the hospital; angry that he couldn't do anything for himself, not even go to the bathroom. Pissed off that Travis had gone and bought a couch that was clearly very expensive. Furious that he was helpless right now and had no idea what the hell was going on. "I didn't need a better couch, or a bigger couch. That other couch was just fine."

Travis, annoying man that he was, refused to be upset by Rod's attitude. He grinned, his stupid teeth white and brilliant. "Quit trying to pick a fight with me. It isn't going to work. I needed a bigger couch, so I found one. Sit down."

Rod had no choice. He lowered himself down. The god damned couch was even more comfortable than it looked. Travis helped him lift his injured leg up onto the cushions and positioned him so he was lying back.

"Trav, we need to talk about what's going on, why you've done all this." Rod tried to make his voice firm and businesslike, but he was pretty sure he sounded whiny and petty.

Travis crouched down by the side of the couch so he was basically eye level with Rod.

"We do." His blue eyes offered a promise Rod was afraid of. It felt like the first time he'd jumped out of a plane, except then he'd been confident he could do it, that the parachute would deploy and he would land safely on the ground. With Travis he didn't know where he would land.

There was a knock on the front door.

"And we will, dammit," Travis muttered as he stood up. "That must be Cameron."

Cameron had left them at the hospital with a cheery wave and a promise to see them later. Rod hadn't realized he meant later that day.

His mind focused on what Travis had been about to say, Rod regarded Travis thoughtfully as he stood and opened the door.

It was Cam and a few other guys. One of the other men was Ira, Cam's artist boyfriend. The second was Marcus, a friend of Cam's who worked with him at the Loft, and the third was Theo-G1988. Rod felt his eyes go extra wide and his cheeks flush. It wasn't as if they had done anything, but—he darted a glance at Travis, who was acting perfectly normal—he felt awkward.

Theo made a beeline for Rod, stepping nimbly through the stacked boxes and other moving paraphernalia.

"Rod, I am so glad to see you are, well, mostly okay." Theo looked him over before starting to sit on the edge of the couch. "I totally invited myself over, but I promise I won't stay. Is this all right?"

Rod nodded, feeling tongue-tied in front of Travis and Cam.

"Let's take a look around," Ira said to Marcus. "You don't mind, do you?"

Rod shook his head and watched the two of them disappear down a hallway to his left. Marcus, as usual, was wearing an outrageous T-shirt, this one fuchsia-toned and emblazoned with "Always forward, never straight."

"Gosh, honestly, I thought maybe you were ghosting me." Theo beamed at Rod, his smile brilliant. "Finally I slunk into the Loft, because I remembered you telling me the only other person you knew in town was the bartender. Cam took pity on me and told me what happened." It occurred to Rod that it might be a good idea to at least let his parents know he'd been in an accident but would recover.

"Hi, I'm Travis Walker." Travis had been watching the exchange but now came over to the couch and stuck out his hand for Theo to shake. A weird expression slithered across his handsome face before he masked it with a smile.

Theo hopped up and shook Travis's hand. All the oxygen

had been sucked from the room. At least, none was making its way into Rod's lungs. He was injured, recovering, far too emotionally vulnerable. Please, please, he begged Theo silently, do not say anything. Rod hadn't known him long enough to gauge if he was a spiller or not.

"Theo Gutierrez." There was a short silence; Travis was waiting for something more. "Uh, new to Skagit, met Rod a month or so ago. Rod's friend Travis, of course. I've heard about you."

Rod winced. This was not what he needed. Opening his eyes, he watched the inevitable train wreck that was his life. Cam was watching with amusement, not cutting in or changing the subject. Traitor.

"Oh?" Travis, who normally looked like the stereotypical All-American guy, put a dangerous edge on the word. Cam disappeared in the direction of the kitchen, following Ira and Marcus. Rod could hear Marcus exclaiming over the size of the yard.

"All good things, of course." Theo's gaze darted over to Rod, who probably looked panicked. On a good day he had a very good poker face, but today was surreal. "Anyway," Theo perched on the edge of the couch again, "quick, give me all the details, and then I will get out of your hair."


TEN MINUTES LATER, Travis was shutting the door after Theo as Ira and Marcus sauntered back into the living room to stand with Cam. Surely it could not have taken that long for them to tour the tiny home. Rod narrowed his eyes at Cam, who grinned and raised one elegant eyebrow in response.

"How was Theo?"

"Theo was fine," Rod muttered, scowling.

"Did big bad Travis scare him off?"

Cam, Ira, and Marcus cracked up, Travis stared at them like they were loons. "You guys are a bunch of comedians."

"All right then, let's see about getting the rest of the furniture inside and set up," Ira announced.

A new couch wasn't the only thing Travis had purchased. There was a coffee table, a table and chairs for the kitchenette, and several large boxes that went in the direction of the bedrooms. Exhaustion overtook Rod. The work his body was doing healing took a lot of energy, plus sleeping in the hospital had been almost impossible. He let his eyes fall shut, barely stirring when a blanket was draped over him as he lay on the couch. He heard quiet whispers and the door opening and closing when the three visitors left, but he was too sleepy to say goodbye.

# 12

Travis paced around the house, impatient for Rod to wake up and scared as shit about his reaction when he did. Travis harbored a tiny shard of uncertainty about Rod's feelings toward him, but if that Theo guy's reaction had been anything to go by, Travis was on the right track. Maybe. To be honest, he didn't know up from down right now. All he did know was, he was going to do everything possible to get Rod to understand he wasn't kidding around. Travis was here to stay.

Seeing Rod huddled on the couch, the yellowing bruises and healing scrapes still covering his body visible because he'd kicked the blanket off with his good leg and his T-shirt had ridden up exposing his abdomen, still terrified Travis. An icy fear had settled deep in his gut as he drove like a man on fire to get to Skagit. It had been like nothing he'd ever experienced.

Regardless of Cam trying to reassure him that the worst was past, Travis had imagined all sorts of terrible things, each worse than the previous. The worst of all was the thought that he might never be able to tell Rod he loved him. That he was a complete and total fool for not recognizing it earlier.

Rod was scruffy, something he generally tried to avoid.

Travis didn't care what Rod looked like; having him alive and whole was what mattered. He'd been complaining that his face itched and the nurse in the hospital couldn't shave right. Travis had promised they would shave the offending scruff off today. His hair had grown out too; normally Rod kept it cut very close to his scalp, but now it was sticking up in uneven clumps. Travis would never tell Rod, but it made him look adorable.

There was nothing like coming far too close to losing Rod, the best person in his life, to make Travis realize he needed to get his ass in gear. Nothing was going to change if he didn't make an effort. Maybe assembling furniture would go toward proving his devotion. Travis snickered quietly as he started to open a box.

After half an hour, Travis gave up trying to follow the instructions for the Ikea entertainment center. He may have graduated top of his class, but the instruction manual was defeating him, possibly because he couldn't focus on it. Collecting the empty boxes, he hauled them out to the side of the house where he broke them down for recycling.

When he came back inside, he knew Rod was awake even though his eyes weren't open. His body was no longer relaxed into sleep.

It was now or never. Travis's palms were sweaty. Jeez, he'd never been this nervous with anyone he'd wanted to be with before. He supposed it had never been this important before.

Rod's dark eyes opened slightly when Travis came through the front door, tracking him as he crossed the room to hover near the couch . Now or never, Travis repeated to himself, now or never.

If Travis had been a betting man, this would be the moment where he pushed all his chips into the middle of the table, *Ocean's 11*–style. He and Rod had watched that movie and its sequels so many times they both knew all the lines.

"What now? You have a look on your face," Rod muttered.

"You were right earlier, we need to talk. But first, I want to do this." Actions speak louder than words. His dad had told him that all his life.

He leaned in—faster than he intended, because he was scared as shit—and brushed his lips against Rod's, nearly smacking him in the teeth. Rod gasped, his lips parting under Travis's own. *Yes!* a victorious voice shouted in his head. Trying to be mindful, he pulled away, intending to ask permission for more. Before he could, Rod grabbed the back of his neck, forcing him closer. Travis slipped to his knees, kissing Rod as he'd never allowed himself to want before.

Rod's lips were a little dry, and his beard was scratchy. None of that stopped Travis from first licking Rod's lips and then delving inside to taste him, to slide his tongue across Rod's, to suck on his plump lower lip. Was there a name for a heaven you didn't know existed but, remarkably, found right in front of you? Maybe. For Travis it was Rod.

He didn't know how much time passed as they explored each other's mouths, surprisingly calm, as if it was something they had been doing forever. The kiss was languid and hot, a mid-August day when the promise of an afternoon thunderstorm loomed. It was home. Lazy and reckless at the same time.

Eventually they broke apart, both breathing hard. Rod looked at him, eyes wide with wonder and a little apprehension.

Travis spoke first. He might as well go big; there was no point in holding back. He brushed a hand across Rod's forehead and healing wounds, then down his cheek, feeling the warmth and vitality that made up his best friend. This was a moment he would never be able to repeat. It needed to be done right. Travis may have been slow on the uptake, but he knew that what happened next was more important than the kiss they'd just shared. "I hope that was okay."

Rod nodded, but Travis saw hesitation in the movement and questions in his eyes.

"Why?"

There was no middle ground where Rod was concerned. Travis couldn't declare "I love you" and then change his mind—if he did, everything between them would be destroyed. There would be no friendship left. Rod gave with his whole heart, Travis understood that. Rod wouldn't try to pepper spray him; he would shut Travis out and never speak to him again.

"I've always loved you, Rod. I didn't recognize it for what it was until recently. You know, sometimes I need things spelled out for me. This was one of those times." He mentally thanked Abigail again for opening his eyes.

"You kissed me," Rod stated.

"Yeah, and you kissed me back."

"You love me?" Rod whispered.

"Yeah, I do. I'm stupid, but I guess you know that."

Rod struggled to sit up, wincing as his bad leg tapped against the floor. Travis shifted and scooped an arm around him so he was sitting up and his leg was carefully propped on the coffee table. Rod patted the couch cushion next to him. Travis squished in as close as he could.

"I don't know what to say," Rod said. "This is weird."

"Why is it weird?"

"It just is. It's one thing to fantasize that the person who's been your best friend forever is going to realize he might possibly be in love with you, and it's another to be sitting next to you on this brand-new couch, my face stinging from whisker burn because we made out for ten minutes."

"Was that ten minutes?"

"Focus, Travis."

"You fantasized about me?"

"Travis."

"Okaaaay." Travis wanted to be done with the talking part and get back to the kissing part. It was going to be incredibly hard (ha-ha) to keep things light while Rod's leg healed. Now that he'd finally kissed Rod, Travis wanted to strip him naked and explore everything about him. He wanted to wake up in the morning with Rod next to him in bed. He wanted everything.

"You found a house. You," Rod swept a hand out at the boxes and furniture in the living room, "bought stuff, permanent stuff. You moved me here—without asking me, which is another conversation—I guess after all this time it's difficult for me to believe?"

"Even when we were kissing just now?"

"When we were kissing, I wasn't thinking about anything. This doesn't feel real. I'm sorry. I think... I don't know." His voice trailed off. "I think I don't know how I feel."

Travis twisted around so he could see Rod's face and Rod could see his. "I will do everything in my power to get you to believe I am for real. That we are for real."

"What about your family? What about the farm? What about all those things that have been important to you for so long?"

"First, you're one of those things that has been important to me for so long. I had it pointed out to me, quite bluntly, by Abs that you've always been there for me. So Abs is good. I've talked to my dad; believe it or not, he's good too. We've got some stuff to work out with the farm, but I think things are going to be okay. Mom..." Travis shook his head, because no way was he going to tell Rod the kinds of things she'd been saying to him. "That's probably about what you'd expect."

"So you're moving to Skagit? That's what all this furniture means?"

"You of all people know how much I've wanted to get away from Walla Walla. Skagit is perfect. Similar size but closer to the big city. And the ocean. The real ocean down south that you can swim in without getting hypothermia," he qualified.

"You've always wanted to go to the ocean. Remember that time you filled a huge bucket with dirt from your mom's garden? I helped you drag it into the bathroom, and we poured the dirt into the tub and filled it with water. I thought Lenore was going to commit murder when she found us 'surfing' in the bathtub." He laughed. "There was mud everywhere."

"One of these days we'll both get to the ocean, for real."

Travis didn't realize how much hope he was putting into those words until he said them out loud—how much he wanted to be sure that their future was together and the ocean would be a place they would visit not just once but many times, even when they were old and gray and couldn't get it up anymore. Well, any more than once a day.

"When you said your mom was reacting 'about as I'd expect,' what exactly did you mean?"

Trust Rod not to let Travis get away with glossing over anything.

"And what happened with Lisa?"

Travis groaned. He did not want to talk about this.

"Tell me."

"Do I get to kiss you again afterward? It's very embarrassing and only highlights my general stupidity."

"Trav."

Travis made the best sad-puppy face he could. Rod rolled his eyes and laughed.

"Yes, we can kiss again. After you tell me."

He let out a huff and pathetically slumped back against the couch cushions.

"After you left, Abs gave me a pretty good talking-to. I'm sorry for putting you through that. You promise we're gonna make out? This isn't pretty."

"We're not if you don't tell me what happened."

"I wanted to break it off with her, but gently, which is hard to do. I would say it's probably impossible. Anyway, I took her home after dinner one night and she started talking about babies and how she wanted to get pregnant right away, and I pretty much told her no way, the wedding was off. It was bad." He left out the part about the pepper spray.

"I'm sorry," Rod said.

"Before she and her dad left on their trip, I apologized again." Travis ran a hand through his hair. "We're definitely not friends, and she's not going to be visiting us anytime soon, but... I tried to make it better."

"And then?"

"And then, what?"

"How come you're here now?"

"No kissing yet?" He pouted again.

"I'm injured. You need to be very careful. Let me think..."

Travis couldn't help but smile while Rod came up with something he knew would be ridiculous.

Rod pointed his elbow at Travis. "You can kiss me there."

Travis wasn't going to argue. He figured he'd probably get permission to kiss more if he was really really good. Gently grasping Rod's biceps, he leaned in and placed a kiss right on the pointy knob. They'd watched *Raiders of the Lost Ark* plenty of times; Travis knew the script here.

Lifting his head, he looked at Rod, who pointed at his ear. Travis leaned closer in, kissing the shell of Rod's ear and then licking it. Loving the sound of Rod's gasp. He couldn't help but nibble a bit before he leaned back and looked at Rod again.

And yeah, now he was pointing at his cheek, with a great big smile that made Travis's heart pound with joy. He placed a chaste kiss on Rod's whiskery cheek. Rod turned his head and sought Travis's mouth, their lips pressing together lightly. Travis was going to pull back, but again Rod placed a hand on his neck, pulling him closer.

It was everything he'd ever imagined about the perfect kiss. It was exactly how a kiss between them was supposed to feel. Mindful of Rod's leg and other injuries, Travis slipped his free hand under Rod's T-shirt, needing to feel his bare skin. He caressed Rod's abs and let his hand wander upward to his furry chest and across one nipple. Rod groaned into his mouth, sucking on Travis's tongue. Travis felt himself getting hard. As much as he didn't want to stop, he knew they had to.

He leaned away, and Rod let his hand slip from Travis's neck. He missed the touch already. They stared at each other for a long moment. Rod's lips were puffy and slightly open in a seeming invitation. God, he wanted to kiss him again, to keep going until they were both satisfied. Travis didn't know what Rod was thinking, but Travis was thinking four weeks of "very light activity" was going to mean a lot of cold showers. Surely in four weeks they could at least give each other hand jobs? Maybe the physical therapist had meant to use four weeks as a guide-line—and maybe sex wasn't included? His heart leapt at the thought.

"This sucks." Rod flopped backward.

"No, it doesn't, but I bet it can if we are very careful." Travis was going to have a chat with Rod's physical therapist.

"Still feels unreal."

"I guess I'll just have to keep proving it's real, then."

## 13

Rod's lips tingled from the kiss. Reflexively, he raised a hand to run a finger across them as if he could feel its echo. Holy cow. He could still feel the weight of Travis's breath against his own, how good it had felt when Travis put his hand on Rod, how quickly his body had reacted regardless of the low-level ache of bone and tissue healing. Just thinking about it was making his cotton boxers tighter.

Rod tried to think of something unpleasant to calm himself down. He probably should call his parents. That did the job.

"Do you think we could replace my phone?" he asked as Travis lugged a box from the living room into the kitchen.

"Of course! We should have done it earlier. I'll be back in a jiffy."

Rod snorted. What self-respecting guy said stuff like, "back in a jiffy"? Travis, apparently, and Rod didn't want him to change.

"Don't get me anything fancy." He narrowed his eyes at Travis to drive home his point.

Travis left, not bothering to acknowledge Rod's instruction. Rod heard the deep rumble of Travis's truck as it started up, then a roar as he gave it some gas before backing out the driveway. Show-off.

Travis was back in under an hour. Rod had spent the time alone turning over the day's events in his mind, trying to make sense of them. Of the kiss, trying to convince himself it was nothing.

"Don't argue with me," Travis said as he dropped the bag on the couch next to Rod.

"What do I need this for? The damn thing could probably control the space station," Rod grumbled as he took the cellophane-wrapped box out of the bag and turned it over in his hands.

"Look, I added you to my account; it was not a big deal. Quit trying to pick a fight. I'm really not going to argue with you about it."

"Fine." It wasn't as if he could return it under his own power, and he needed to make some calls. Pressing the power button, he updated the phone and familiarized himself with the interface. Eventually there was no reason to procrastinate any longer. He tapped in his dad's cell number and counted seven rings before he started to wonder if his dad had changed the number and not told him. The thought that one or both of his parents would fade permanently from his life had occurred to him before, there was so little binding them together.

"Hello?" The warm rumble of his dad's deep voice caught him off guard.

"Hi, Dad."

"Rodney, how are you? You have a new phone number?"

Rod's chest clenched. The sound of his dad's voice hit him somewhere dark and secret that still wanted to be his dad's boy. Rod hadn't realized he missed him... even if he did hate being called Rodney. He and his dad had never been super close; there weren't any father-son camping trips as a teen, but Rod had early memories of laughter and sunshine. As he grew older, it seemed like the three of them—himself, his mom, and his dad—had been awkward intruders in their own lives, play-acting at what a family was supposed to be like. He still didn't understand why they'd waited until he was in college to split up.

"Yeah, my old phone got kinda bashed up."

As he sat on the very comfortable new couch, watching Travis move in and out of various spaces rearranging boxes and furniture, Rod told his dad about the accident and what he was looking at in terms of recovery.

"The doctor says as long as I follow instructions I should heal pretty well."

In the background of the call there were family noises: the clatter of dishes, a kid or teen yelling something, a dog barking. Rod knew his dad's wife had a couple of kids, but Rod had never met them. The wedding had been at a time Rod had found inconvenient, so he hadn't bothered to go. Now he wondered who he'd been punishing, his dad or himself. Yeah, his dad had been weird when Rod came out, but it wasn't as if he'd publicly shunned him or banned him from his new life.

"So ya know, Dad, Travis and I have moved in together."

"You two have been friends for a long time. He's in Skagit with you now?"

"We moved in together, as in together-together." Even if it had only been *today*, and his heart of hearts was suspicious as to whether Travis was truly staying or not, Rod was willing to trot that out to his dad.

"You're both gay?" The sound in the background stopped, and Rod wondered where his dad was and who might have been listening.

"Travis is bi, not that it makes any difference."

"No, I don't suppose it does. Together, huh?" His dad was quiet.

The horrifying realization crossed Rod's mind that he had never once told his dad about any guy he dated. No wonder his few boyfriends gave up on him; they had been mere placeholders, not even meriting mention to his parents.

His dad started to say something, and then there was a muffled rustling sound, his dad probably putting his hand over the mic. Rod waited, wondering what kind of bomb he'd set off this time. Surely his dad understood that if Rod was gay it meant he would be with a man? There was sound again, but this time a different voice came over the line.

"Rod?" He didn't recognize the woman's voice, although he had a good idea who it was. "I hope you don't mind, I wrestled the phone from your dad. This is Meg; we've never met, but I'd really like to meet you. *We'd* really like to meet you."

"Um, sure?" He wasn't sure how to respond to this unexpected overture. As far as he knew, Meg wasn't a charter member of PFLAG. Of course, since he hadn't bothered to get to know her at all, how would he know?

"We all would like to meet you, Rod. Morgan and Alex and I." There was a pause; Rod heard voices that must have been Morgan and Alex in the background fighting over something, but Rod couldn't tell what. "One of the few things your dad and I have disagreed about is you. I've been bugging Will to reach out, but he was being stubborn. He thought maybe you didn't want to talk to him."

"We haven't talked in a while; maybe we never talked, I don't know." God, he sounded like a dick. There had been so much silence in his house growing up. Maybe that was why he'd gravitated to Travis's, where there was always noise and activity. He heard the dog bark in the background again and felt a stab of jealousy. He'd never been allowed to have a pet of any kind: goldfish, puppy, kitten, pet rock... the answer had always been no.

There was some whispering, then silence as the phone was muffled again, and then Meg's voice was back. "We'd like to come visit one of these weekends, if that would be okay. Will is terrible at expressing his feelings—understatement of the year; I'm sure the only reason he said yes when I asked him on a date was from pure shock—but he's missed you."

Had he missed his dad? It's hard to miss something you never thought you had. Rod missed the idea of family, not the real thing. "Really? I find that kind of hard to believe."

An almost inaudible sigh. "Your father's story isn't mine to tell. He's standing next to me nodding. I'm going to hand the phone back over to him. I hope to meet you soon."

There was a pause, and the sound of a deep breath. Rod wondered if his dad was nervous. And then his voice.

"Rodney—Rod, I forgot, you prefer Rod. Um, a phone conversation isn't really the way I imagined this, but I suppose, Band-Aids and all. Your mother and I, well, it wasn't until after you started school that I realized how bad a match we were, how little we had in common. I tried to talk to her, but she refused to consider divorce, and I was brought up to believe that we don't always get happiness—that sometimes you need to live with the hand you were dealt, so I did.

"You seemed happy whether I was there or not, so I spent as much time away from home as I could, taking every promotion, every travel opportunity. It wasn't until I met Meg that I understood how unhappy I was."

The words were rushing one over the other in a torrent. How long had his dad wanted to say this, Rod wondered. He didn't remember his grandparents except as a much-older couple who had little time for children; they were to be "seen and not heard." His grandfather had always worn a button-down shirt and tie, his grandmother a demure skirt and sweater set when visiting. They were shadowy, stern figures who'd never joked or laughed with him. While the mood in the Beton home growing up had never been jovial, his grandparents' visits had been repressive. In hindsight it explained a lot about his dad.

"When I insisted on divorce, you of course had already left for college. It's hard for me to believe I let myself, all of us, be miserable for eighteen years." A rueful laugh. "I didn't know it could be different. Anyway, I'd lost my chance with you. I vowed to do better with Meg's kids. One day I told her that and, well, Meg has a temper." Another chuckle. "Anyway, she helped me to understand that I owed it to both of us to at least try to fix things with you. I know it's too late for T-ball and whatnot, but if—I'd like to prove myself a better father to you."

"What about me being gay?"

"Rod, there is nothing wrong with love. Whether it is same-sex or heterosexual, the important thing is to love without holding back. This is what I have learned. I'm sorry I did such a poor job of it while you were growing up. But if you love some-one, you have to love them fiercely enough to fight for it. I never did with your mother."

"But you do with Meg?"

"Yes, and I know I haven't proved it to you, but I love you too."

To love without holding back. The words ricocheted around. Rod half listened to his dad while he tested himself against that standard and concluded he had never loved without holding back. Loving honestly meant being open to hurt, and he had always guarded his heart.

Something needed to change.

As they ended the call, Meg interrupted again, wrangling his new address out of him with a promise that he would be seeing them in the next few weeks. He clicked off, feeling a bit like he'd been hit by a car. Again.

Rod called his mother next, but she didn't answer. He left a message. The conversation with his dad resonated. He wondered if his mother had found a better way to love or if she had just moved on to the next person she found.

TRAVIS RETURNED from the back of the house, where he'd been doing something that involved muffled swearing. His hair was messy and he looked sweaty. Rod wanted to climb him like a pole. Damn his stupid leg. Damn Travis's timing, damn Rod himself for being wary. Damn him for not knowing how to lower the wall he'd built around himself without ever being aware it was happening.

Part of him was celebrating like mad, wanting to toss caution aside and accept what Travis offered with complete abandon. The distrustful half of himself had spent too long watching Travis with other people. The men he chose when they were away from town, and the women when he was home. That dark side kept whispering that this wouldn't last, that Travis would prove to be fickle and drop Rod as soon as a difficult decision came up or other real-life things interfered. Like Rod's dad and stepmom coming to visit.

"Wanna come see?" Travis asked.

"See what?"

"The bedroom. Come on, I'll help you."

As Travis half carried Rod toward the back of the house, Rod wondered, not for the first time since they arrived that morning, where all the boxes had come from. He'd only moved a few months ago, and all his stuff had fit into the back of his truck.

"How come there's so much stuff?"

Travis glanced around but kept them both moving toward the short hallway. "My dad dropped off most of my stuff yesterday."

Rod tried to stop their forward momentum, but Travis was an unmovable force—or maybe a moving one.

"Your dad was here?" His voice squeaked. Everything that had happened since he'd been released from the hospital continued to make Rod's mind boggle.

"Yeah, he says he'll say hi the next time he's in town. He didn't want to intrude, and he had to get back anyway. He's a little worried Mom is going to do something wacked. To be honest, I was worried she might drag everything of mine out the back patio and pour gasoline on it."

They arrived at one of two open doors. Travis maneuvered him so he could see inside the room. Against the opposite wall, underneath a nice-size window, there was a king bed taking up most of the room, a bedside table on each side. The bed was made up with deep blue sheets with a comforter of the same color thrown over them and several pillows. To the left of the bed was a closet with boxes stacked in it, but what Travis was really showing him was the huge TV and entertainment center he'd mounted on the wall across from the bed.

On each bedside table there were game controllers. His and his, Rod snorted to himself.

"Just while you're healing up. Then we can move the system out to the living room—or not. Here, let's get you in bed."

The couch had been perfectly comfortable, and it was only eight in the evening, but Rod grudgingly admitted that lying down sounded great. Amazing, even. Moving from the hospital to the house and everything else had tired him out. Travis helped him lie back and then elevated his bad leg on a top of a bunch of throw pillows Rod was sure he'd never seen before.

Rod's stomach rumbled loudly enough that Travis heard it.

"Damn, one of us is going to have to learn how to cook. There's some kind of fancy grocery store a couple blocks away with premade stuff. I'll go grab us some dinner." Before he left the room, Travis turned on the TV. *Twister* was playing. "This okay?"

Of course it was okay. Travis knew Rod loved disaster movies, the more terrible the better. The front door shut behind Trav, and the house was quiet except for the impending doom playing on the fifty-two-inch screen.

When Travis returned, Rod's favorite scene was on. Travis plopped the grocery bag on the bed and sat on the edge to watch with him.

"Oh, the drive-in is about to get wiped off the planet!" They watched together as Jack Torrance's face shattered and disappeared under the force of the tornado.

"Did you know they used the sound of a camel moaning as a sound effect?" Travis asked him.

"Dude, I *told* you that."

"Still my favorite scene."

"In this movie or favorite ever?"

This was an ongoing argument between them. Until *Sharknado*, *Twister* had been Rod's favorite bad disaster movie. Travis favored *Volcano*. Rod thought he just had the hots for a younger Tommy Lee Jones, something Rod didn't really have a case against.

"Quit trying to start an argument with me. I brought food."

Rod devoured the roast beef sandwich and potato salad. The sandwich was just how he liked it, with extra mustard and cheddar. Travis sat next to him wolfing down his own meal while they watched the end of the movie.

"It's totally ridiculous that they get back together, just saying," Trav grumbled.

"Yeah."

Rod's eyelids were too heavy to keep open any longer. Now that his belly was full, there was nothing to keep him from going to sleep.

Except Travis leaned over and kissed him again. His eyes flew open. Travis's guileless blue eyes stared into his own. Rod felt like he could be drowning and Trav's lips pressed against his were breathing hope into the depth of his soul, a delicate frisson that Rod was helpless against and didn't want to fight.

Trav pulled back and Rod groaned, missing the touch already.

"Yeah, I'm sleeping on the couch," Travis said. "I don't trust myself not to crush your leg in my sleep."

"What?" Rod whined.

Trav stood, adjusting himself. Rod was spitefully glad Travis was as aroused as he was; now they would both have a hard time going to sleep.

"Sweet dreams." Travis kissed him quickly on the forehead before he left the room.

## 14

---

Travis pulled into the parking lot of the upscale grocery store. It was packed with cars and trucks, and he had to hunt around for a spot before finally finding one at the very back. It was a good thing Rod was at physical therapy; Travis would feel guilty making him walk this far.

Rod was healing on pace, but he was bored. Travis was trying to help him stay busy but, well, it was hard enough staying out of their bed. Or it *would* be their bed, once Rod got the cast off, but Travis wasn't doing anything to set him back.

He locked his truck and headed across the parking lot to the store. There were a few small white tents set up outside. One had a vendor with all sorts of early spring veggies, some cut up for customers to sample. There were also jars containing sauces he assumed were either made from the veggies or for the veggies. And there were several cookbooks.

He picked up the cookbook and flipped through it. The pictures were beautiful, but it was like reading a foreign language. He put it back down.

The older lady behind the counter smiled at him. "Not a foodie?"

"A foodie?"

She waved a hand. "A person who likes to experiment with different kinds of ingredients, that sort of thing."

He laughed. "I can barely cook the ingredients I know about. I'm not sure I'm ready for anything more than sandwiches." Although, to be honest, he *was* getting tired of sandwiches. Rod hadn't complained, but Travis thought he'd probably appreciate something different.

"Cooking isn't that hard. It's much easier than baking. It's harder to experiment when the ingredients need to be precisely measured."

Maybe it was her nonjudgmental tone or her use of the word experiment that had Travis picking up the cookbook again.

"Are these your recipes?"

"Not all of them. Several of us who sell at the farmers market on a regular basis got together and collaborated, and this book is the result. Our main goal was to promote local ingredients. Things that a regular person could find at the market or grocery store in season. A small attempt to lessen our reliance on iceberg lettuce from California and things like that."

He bought the book. Then he went to check out the other tent where a vendor had several different kinds of fresh-caught fish and shellfish displayed on ice. There was also fish jerky (which sounded gross to him) and a stand of recipe cards. He chatted with that vendor too, although cooking fish was something he didn't feel quite ready for.

Inside the store, Travis wandered around the fresh and local sections, taking stock of what they carried. He picked a recipe out of his new book and found all the ingredients for it. Once he studied the recipes, he realized she was right. They weren't that difficult. If he approached it like an experiment, like those he'd done while in college, the process wouldn't be as daunting.

On the way to pick up Rod at the mall, Travis took the long

way around Skagit. Originally Skagit had been a timber town, and then the farmers had come in. Most of the big farms seemed to be root vegetables, but he also saw fields of cabbage and broccoli, as well as tulips and daffodils. There was a vibrant farming community in the area. Different from wheat, but not that different.

As he waited for Rod, he called and left a message for his dad. Then he called a local real estate agent and set up a time to talk about what he was looking for.

An indistinct figure pushed out of the doorway. Even though he couldn't see his features, Travis knew it was Rod. Emotion Travis wasn't used to yet welled, and he had to take a few deep breaths. Every time he circled back to the thought that he could have lost Rod forever, either in the car accident or because he was too clueless to know what he had, it felt like he'd barely missed falling off a ledge.

Rod was smiling, which Travis loved; a half-hitched, mischievous smile. Travis wondered what he was thinking. He hopped out of the truck and went around to open the door. Rod still needed assistance getting into the cab, something he bitched about every single time. And every time Rod bitched, Travis was thankful that he was able to. That he'd woken up from the accident, that he hadn't lost his leg—although they would have dealt with that too.

"What're you smiling about?" Rod grumbled as Travis helped him up.

"I'm smiling because you were smiling. What were you smiling about?" Travis tossed Rod's crutches in the back seat.

"I've made a friend. Her name is Gloria, and she is hilarious. Don't worry, she has to be in her eighties, and even if she was younger, I don't swing that way."

"Ha, ha, ha. Very funny." Travis would never admit he felt jealous for a millisecond.

"Anyway, she says hi and that she'd love to meet you. I think she's kind of bored. She lives in an assisted living facility, and it sounds like she is a lot more active than most of the residents."

"WHAT'S THIS?" Rod looked at the dish Travis had plunked down on the table.

Travis, who been solely focused on following the directions so the recipe would come out somewhat like it was supposed to, felt suddenly shy. "Ratatouille?"

Rod grinned, catching his wrist before he could slink back into the kitchen. "It looks delish. You made it yourself?"

"Yeah. Let me grab the bread from the oven."

Rod didn't let go. "Kiss me."

Such a simple request made Travis's heart sing.

"Isn't it supposed to be the other way around?" He remembered his dad having a goofy apron he wore when he grilled that had "Kiss the Cook" screen-printed on it.

"If the cook would bring his ass over here so I could kiss him…" Rod raised an eyebrow.

Travis bent to meet Rod's upturned lips. As with most things they did, the kiss started out sweet but quickly turned hot. Travis had to step away. He adjusted himself through his jeans.

"You are dangerous."

"I do my best."

## 15

"Mall walking?" Rod had asked. After three weeks of physical therapy, the physical therapist suggested he go mall walking.

"Yes, mall walking," Dana repeated with a great deal of patience. "The floor is level, and there are lots of benches to sit on when you get tired. You can work up your endurance with the seniors who do the same."

There was only one mall in Skagit. Rod had managed to avoid it at all costs, and now his physical therapist wanted him to go there on purpose.

"You're making great progress. If you want to continue in a safe environment, the mall is the perfect place to do it. You can slowly increase your distance and weight on your leg as the doc allows—and stay out of the rain."

Spring may have come to Skagit, but somebody in management hadn't gotten the memo. It had been raining almost nonstop since Rod came home. He was housebound anyway, but the rain made it worse and made him even crankier.

The first week or so he'd been perfectly happy to lie in bed watching movies and catching up on the sleep he didn't get in the hospital. Travis kept busy organizing the house, watching TV with Rod, and teaching himself how to cook via YouTube videos. He was in and out of the house all day. He was wherever Rod needed him to be, except in bed.

So add horny as fuck to the list of things that were making Rod irritable. Since the first day home when Travis had... *declared himself* to Rod, everything had been hands-off. Travis was still sleeping on the formerly brand-new couch. Rod was starting to hate that couch. He remembered, during sleepovers as kids, often waking up to find Travis completely trapped by his blanket. He'd fought the blanket and the blanket won. Now Rod didn't care if Travis was a blanket hog: he belonged in bed next to Rod.

They'd exchanged kisses, too chaste for Rod's liking, Travis brushing his lips across Rod's cheek when he brought him coffee or dinner. Then there was Travis's warm palm at Rod's back, supporting him as he made his way to the kitchen or bathroom. Rod's pessimistic side was starting to give way to hope, and horniness. Giving way was an understatement. It was more like a landslide.

"When can I have sex?"

Dana laughed.

"What's so funny?"

"Oh I always have a little bet with myself over how long until the sex question comes up. Of course it depends on the patient. You've lasted way past my estimate. I lost to myself."

Rod glowered at her. She just laughed again and smirked at him. Over the past few weeks of therapy they had become friends of a sort. While Rod wasn't going to miss PT, he would miss Dana.

"As far as your leg goes, still no direct weight on it. Keep it elevated when you are at home; you can lie on your side or back." She flipped through his chart, thick with papers. It was a good thing he had medical insurance through work. Anything not covered by the other driver's insurance was mostly taken care of. Still, he didn't look forward to the final bill.

"Your lung has healed very well. As with anything, start out slow and see how you feel. I don't recommend any acrobatics, but you should be okay. And maybe a little less grouchy." She snickered.

"Anybody ever complain about your bedside manner?"

"Nope!" Dana said cheerfully.

THE FIRST TIME, Travis went with him to the mall, "just to make sure nothing happens, all right?" He hung around like a mother hen, constantly asking him how he felt, if he was tired. Rod was, but if he didn't keep up the physical therapy his leg would take longer to recover. And if he hadn't needed his crutches for balance he would've seriously considered using them as a weapon.

The second time he went, Rod made Travis promise to leave after helping him out of the truck and inside. Rod felt like he'd been moody the past few days. He blamed it on being hopelessly horny. Travis was still being his normal cheerful self, which only made Rod grumpier. Dana had said they could have sex, so why hadn't he told Travis? He was irritating himself. A nice sweaty drag up and down the mall would serve him right.

Today Rod was clumping his way from the far end of the mall to the food court, trying to beat an octogenarian just ahead of him. Gloria was fifty feet ahead, and there was no way he was catching up with her. Dana had told him that the best time to come was in the morning before all the stores opened up. It seemed like many seniors in Skagit came to walk the mall in the mornings. He slowly passed a T-shirt shop, heading for the coffee shop at the very end of the food court. One more circuit and he would be done. He had forty minutes before Travis would check in on him.

The food court was a standard design: a large open space with kiosks around the edges and tables for patrons to sit at in the middle. Rod wanted a coffee; it was his reward for already doing two laps and planning on a third. The kid behind the counter watched him approach.

"Hey Rod, how ya doing today? Did you beat the mayor yet?"

"No, she must have boosters on her walker."

From the other side of the food court he heard, "Young man, I am faster than you. Get used to it."

Rod grinned. Gloria Browning and he had hit it off when they met at the mall. She'd been his walking companion since the first day he limped out onto the polished mall floor. Well into her eighties, she'd lived in Skagit her entire life and had hilarious stories to tell. She had been the first female mayor of Skagit in the 1970s, proudly serving for twelve years. The first time he'd been at the mall, pissed off and sweating from exertion like it was ninety degrees instead of a nicely controlled seventy-two, Gloria had challenged him to "get cracking," chuckling as she passed him with her colorfully decorated walker.

The barista finished Rod's coffee and was kind enough to venture from behind the counter and deliver it to the table where Gloria was already waiting for him, damn her. Rod clomped after him with his stupid crutches.

"I see you're in a fine humor this morning, young man."

"I'm really not."

"Poor boy. Are you taking your temper out on your gentleman friend?" She patted the seat next to her. Rod eased himself down. The soft cast allowed for some movement, but not enough for quick sitting or standing. And he got to enjoy it for another eight weeks. Less than initially predicted, but longer than he'd hoped.

Somehow Gloria had managed to weasel who Travis was out of Rod. The woman would have made a great spy. She was bound and determined to make sure the two of them got their happy ending. Rod was still wondering how he'd ended up telling her the long story of their friendship and now more-than-friendship.

Instead of drinking his coffee right away and getting back to walking, the two of them started swapping stories. Rod's were about firefighting and growing up in a small farming town; Gloria's about what it was like in the sixties and seventies in Skagit and how the city had changed. Rod watched the early birds come in and out of the food court. Some walked with purpose; some were just trying to stay out of the rain.

He wasn't sure what it was that caught his eye, but his attention focused on a small figure sitting at one of the tables. The kid had been walking around aimlessly, dragging one hand along tables, wandering up to kiosk storefronts and back to the tables again, before they finally sat down and put their head on their arms.

Mall security had been watching and began to make their way toward the table. The facility had a strict "No loitering unless you pay for something" policy, and it was obvious that this kid was in violation. Every day Rod had been mall walking, the security force had been out and about ensuring the safety and happiness of the paying customers.

Gloria followed his gaze as the guard arrived at the table. The kid raised his head, and in that instant Rod realized he knew that coat and the little person who was wearing it. What was Jasper doing at the mall on a school day?

"I know that kid, his name is Jasper. Jasper Ransom, he rides my bus."

"Do you know him well enough to help him? He looks like he could use a friend."

"Yeah, but god dammit, Gloria, you're faster than I am."

"Ha, I knew it!"

Gloria stood, grabbed her walker, and burned some serious rubber toward the other table. She was halfway there before Rod was up and had his crutches properly positioned. He made his way over slowly and carefully.

Gloria sat herself down next to a panicked and forlorn Jasper. He looked like he'd been living on the streets. Maybe he had. His clothing was dirty, and his face was grubby in a way that seemed like more than that he just forgot to wash it. His hair was tangled; one side was sticking out, and the other possibly had gum or tree sap in it. He was wearing his coat, but it was smeared with dirt too; his sneakers had holes in the toes.

"Hey, Jasper," Rod softly called out as he approached the table.

Jasper turned toward the sound of Rod's voice. Rod watched recognition flood across his face just before he burst into tears. Jasper bolted toward him, and Rod steeled himself for impact, hoping his leg could take it. Gloria grabbed the back of Jasper's jacket, stopping him in his tracks.

"Hang on a second, young man, you'll put your friend back in the hospital. Let him sit down first." She turned to the security guard. "We've got this, thank you."

Whether it was her tone of voice, the majestic sweep of her hand, or because her reputation preceded her, the guard aimed one last suspicious glance at the three of them and ambled off, his attention caught by two high school–aged kids with skateboards.

Rod lowered himself into the uncomfortable plastic chair as Gloria released her grip on Jasper's jacket, allowing him to continue on his trajectory to Rod's side. Jasper sagged against him, sobbing into the front of Rod's shirt, his small body shaking with the force of his tears. Jasper was trying to say something, but Rod couldn't understand what it was through the snot.

"Hey, hey. It's okay, whatever happened, it's okay. Can you calm down and tell me and Gloria what's going on? Come on, take a breath." Rod rocked the boy back and forth, whispering promises he hoped he would be able to keep into Jasper's ear. Rod tried not to breathe in too deeply; Jasper hadn't bathed in a while.

Rod kept rocking back and forth, automatically crooning nonsense words to the little boy, while Gloria watched with concern. Finally Jasper's gasping sobs slowed enough for Rod to ask, "Hey little guy, where's your—" It occurred to Rod he didn't know who Jasper lived with, and he'd never heard Jasper mention an adult. He forged ahead anyway. "—your mom or dad?"

This caused a fresh round of tears, and Gloria shot him another look full of worry. The mall stores were starting to open up. There was a steady stream of people entering now, and Rod felt exposed and uncertain of what to do next. He didn't know anything about Jasper, not really. And Gloria knew even less. He recalled his long-ago conversation with the Yew Elementary secretary and the lunch lady and sighed. He hated being right. Something was going on with Jasper, and dammit, Rod was going to figure out what it was.

Not knowing who else to call, Rod called Travis to come get them. "Them" included Gloria, who claimed they needed her along and there was nothing to look forward to at the assisted living home except chicken piccata for lunch, "and it's bound to be dry because the 'chef' is on vacation and his replacement can't cook his way out of a wet paper bag."

With a little twisting around, Rod was able to pull Jasper up onto his lap. He was probably violating all sorts of rules and regulations about lost children, but who the fuck cared? Jasper felt small under his arm, and Rod wondered when he had last had a good meal. The world was a fucked-up place for a nine-year-old kid to be wandering around hungry, no one paying any attention except to chase him away. He recognized he was furious and made a conscious effort to shove his feelings aside; Jasper didn't need Rod's anger right now.

After what seemed like an eternity, but in reality was the fifteen minutes it took to make the trip from their house to the mall, Rod spotted Travis's truck pulling up into the loading zone outside the food court doors.

"Come on." He lifted Jasper off his lap. "Our ride's here."

"YOUNG MAN, how on earth am I supposed to get up into that thing?" Gloria glared at Travis's monster truck. She shifted her glare to Travis himself.

"Same way I've been getting in, a Travis Walker assist," Rod answered.

Travis rolled his eyes. "Rod knows perfectly well," Travis demonstrated by first opening the front passenger cab door and then the back passenger door, "that there is a step that automatically comes out, see? Who's sitting where?"

Rod allowed Travis to half lift him into the back seat. Jasper insisted on sitting next to Rod. Travis helped Gloria into the front seat.

"So, pretty lady, where are we taking you today?" Travis made sure Gloria's seat belt was fastened. Rod did the same for Jasper.

"Flattery will get you everywhere." Gloria waggled her eyebrows and gave Travis a pat on the shoulder. "I'm part of the A-team today. Our friend here may need a helping hand, and *that* is something I have connections for."

## 16

T ravis herded everyone into the house. Rod guided the little boy—Jasper, he'd called him—to the couch where he leaned his crutches against the wall before sitting down. Jasper whispered something Travis couldn't hear.

Rod looked over at Travis, pointing with his chin toward the kitchen. "We have a hungry kid here; do you think you could rustle up something?"

"I could probably do that. Jasper?"

The little boy looked at him warily, his face filthy and smeared with god knew what. Travis wanted to toss him in the bathtub. He had nothing against dirt, having been a small boy himself once, but the couch was new, and he had plans for it. Plans that didn't involve a great deal of dirt and grime.

"Are we talking cowboy breakfast hungry, or will mac and cheese do?"

Travis hoped Jasper would pick mac and cheese, because he had no idea what a cowboy breakfast would be. He'd been making things out of the cookbook and watching videos online, but the learning curve was steep when most everything he'd cooked until recently was sandwiches and chili from a can. He kept getting thrown off by terms he'd never heard of like "al dente" and "blanch."

Jasper mumbled something again and Rod repeated, louder, "Mac and cheese."

Mac and cheese couldn't be that hard. Of course, the kind he'd made before came out of a box, and they didn't have that. A quick recipe search was overwhelming. Apparently mac and cheese was a *thing*. Whatever. He grabbed a package of pasta from the cabinet and filled a pot with water. There was some cheddar cheese in the fridge; he grated a hefty pile while he waited for the water to boil.

When he reemerged from the kitchen, Gloria was on the phone and Rod was trying to convince Jasper to take a bath.

"Little man, you need to clean up."

Jasper wore a mulish expression that did not bode well. Looked like Rod the Kid Whisperer had his hands full.

Gloria put her hand over the phone's mouthpiece. "Honey, we'll let Maureen worry about that." Then she went back to giving someone instructions to the house.

"Who's Maureen?"

"A friend of Gloria's who has an emergency foster care license." Rod put an arm around Jasper's shoulders and hugged him tightly. "Jasper's had a hard time and been doing a great job taking care of himself, but now he's going to let us help. Except for a bath."

"I want to stay here!" Jasper wailed, tears making tracks down his grubby cheeks.

Rod smiled down at his small friend. "I know you do, buddy. Maybe we can make that happen, but first let's go through the right people, okay? It sounds like Gloria's friend is a cool person who can take care of you."

"Will you go with me and make sure?"

"We'll all go with you, okay? And I'll make sure Maureen has my phone number. And since I'm still healing up, I'm free to come and visit and stuff."

"I'm hungry."

Travis put the bowl of pasta with melted cheese on the table in the eating area. Jasper slid off the couch but waited for Rod to join him instead of coming right over.

"Have you ever made mac and cheese before?" Rod asked Travis.

"Only the kind that's bright orange." Travis shrugged.

Jasper sat down and pulled the bowl close to the edge of the table to peer into it. "This doesn't look like mac and cheese." He poked at it with his fork. "I guess it looks kind of like it. My mom's friend makes really good mac and cheese," he said sadly as he forked a bite into his mouth, making a face. Who knew that a nine-year-old could be so opinionated about pasta and cheese?

"Yeah? Who's your mom's friend?" Rod asked.

While Travis eavesdropped from the kitchen, Rod and Gloria pieced together a timeline from what Jasper told them, although it was a somewhat fractured account. Jasper and his mom had moved "sort of" recently from the place where Rod used to pick him up to a new place, and he was supposed to start school there, but he hadn't. The house had a lot of people living in it. Jasper and his mom shared a room until she'd gone somewhere and hadn't come back. How long ago that was, Jasper didn't really know, but one of the other people told Jasper that his mom didn't pay rent or buy food for him, so he wasn't allowed to stay. Jasper had snuck food from the fridge and stayed in their room until the other people had gotten angry with him. He'd run out of the house and ended up at the mall; the smell of all the food there had made him so hungry.

"He's a friend of Mommy's from work." Another bite,

followed by another. Travis must have missed who "he" was, but Jasper's statement seemed to make sense to Rod.

"Where did your mom work?" Rod asked.

"Mlkfaln," Jasper mumbled around an enormous bite.

"Let the kid eat, Rod, obviously he's decided it isn't poisonous."

"Not as good as Dany's," Jasper said, shoveling pasta into his mouth.

Travis wanted to know what this Dany person did to have a nine-year-old raving about his cooking.

"All right, Maureen, we'll see you and the rest of the posse in a few minutes." Gloria ended her phone conversation and turned to the three of them. "Maureen James and a coworker of hers are on their way. They are going to need to ask Jasper some questions. Jasper is lucky; she has space right now and is looking forward to meeting him. Also, a police detective will be coming to hear what you have to say." Now she was speaking directly to Jasper. "Maureen is the best. She has helped a lot of boys and girls like you."

Jasper lost it again, throwing the fork down and attaching himself to Rod. "No," he sobbed, "no, no, no. I want my mom."

Rod did his singsong talk, rocking Jasper back and forth as he cried.

Travis frowned, meeting Gloria's concerned gaze and not liking her expression: there was something else here. This wasn't just a case of a kid who'd run away. She shook her head at him, mouthing "Later."

"Hey," Rod said, "while we're waiting, let's think of what Todd Toad and Phabian Frog would do. Do you remember them?"

A muffled "Yeah."

"Well? What would they do?"

"They're not real."

"No, they're not real, but sometimes telling stories helps people solve problems, and sometimes it's just for fun. Come on, we can call this one the 'Macaroni Mission.'"

Jasper sat up, looking from Rod to Travis to the half-eaten bowl of what Travis had thought was acceptable mac and cheese. It had pasta and it had cheese.

"They learn to make macaroni?" Jasper used his fork to pick through the remaining food in the bowl.

"That's exactly what they do. What do you think happens?"

As Rod kept Jasper occupied playing food critic, Travis went to talk to Gloria.

"You know something," he said quietly.

Gloria shook her head again, but this time it was in sadness. Her eyes filled with tears. "Early this morning, or late last night, the body of a young woman was discovered under the pier. Police are only just beginning the investigation, but I have a bad feeling. Maureen says a few days ago someone reported Belinda Ransom missing; she hadn't shown up for work in several days, and a coworker became concerned," Gloria was whispering, "because she's a single mother and he saw her car parked only a few blocks from work."

"The pier where the Waterline is?" Travis hadn't been there yet, but the Waterline was a high-end (for Skagit) restaurant that locals and visitors alike flocked to. "Shi—oot."

From across the room, he and Gloria listened to Rod and Jasper as they concocted an adventure for the amphibious explorers involving much better macaroni than Travis had made, but they got so dirty making it they had to take a bath. Travis thought adding the bath element was pushing it, but Jasper didn't object.

A knock on their front door signaled the arrival of several people Travis didn't know.

One was a hulking blond police detective; his badge said S.

Jorgensen. An older woman who made herself known as Maureen James was accompanied by a young boy named Kon who was, and Travis was confused about this, her assistant. And a big black wolflike dog that obeyed every command Kon gave.

Maureen held her hand out to Travis. "Hello, you must be one of the young men who helped Jasper. Gloria told me that Jasper might need a little convincing. Kon does great PR. And so does Xena." Xena wagged her tail but stayed sitting where she was.

Maureen and Detective Jorgensen introduced themselves to Jasper and Rod. Travis suspected Jorgensen was one of those big guys who looked tough but was really a teddy bear. Something in his demeanor told Travis that Jorgensen did not use his size as a weapon.

Rod and Maureen explained to Jasper that the detective and the still-to-arrive social worker wanted to hear what had happened, how he'd come to be at the mall. Jorgensen sat down next to Jasper. Before anything else, he pulled a bright-orange stuffed tiger out of a bag and offered it to Jasper.

"This is my special tiger. I don't usually bring him with me, but I thought maybe you'd like to meet him."

Jasper took the small stuffed animal and looked at it, turning it over in his hands. "What's his name?"

Jorgensen frowned. "Hmmm, he doesn't have a name. Would you like to give him one? He'd probably like that."

It seemed there was more than one child whisperer in the house.

"Umm..." Jasper fiddled with the tiger's soft ears and petted it. "Stripey?"

Jorgensen regarded the tiger seriously before answering, "I think he likes that. Stripey it is."

The social worker arrived a few minutes later. The next hour was controlled chaos with so many people in the house. After reams of paperwork had been signed and signed again, Jasper left a little less reluctantly than Travis had feared, accompanied by Maureen, Kon, and Xena. Rod promised over and over that he would come visit as soon as he could, and that Jasper could call him, because Maureen had his number. Travis wondered how much of this was actually going to happen, but the social worker didn't say it couldn't.

Finally Travis shut the door behind everyone and leaned back against it. The house was eerily quiet with everyone gone. Detective Jorgensen had kindly offered to take Gloria home; they knew each other, it seemed, and the detective said it would be easy for him to give her a ride.

On the way out the door he'd thanked Rod for acting as he had, for stepping up in a difficult situation. "Not everyone does. I'd hate to think if Jasper had been found by someone else or had to spend the night outside." Then he turned and assisted Gloria to his vehicle.

Gloria had kissed both Rod and Travis on the cheek, promising to see them soon. "I'll teach you to cook, young man; I don't know what the two of you have been living on. If you're not busy Saturday morning, there's a social I'd like to miss, and we can go grocery shopping." Travis nodded. It seemed arguing with her would be futile.

Rod was still standing at the front window staring out at the street, though all the cars were gone. A lone neighbor was walking their dog, waiting patiently while the dog happily stopped at every hedge, clump of grass, and lamppost to gather (and leave) scents to dream about. Travis wondered if Rod would want a dog. Rod caught Travis watching him.

"What?" Rod asked.

"What, what?"

"Why are you looking at me like that?"

"Because every single day I discover something else amazing

about you. I thought I knew you, since we've been best friends forever, but I didn't know how amazing you really are." It seemed like all his life he'd been looking at Rod from a very specific angle. Now the view had changed, and all the things he'd taken for granted were fresh and new with different meanings than they'd had before.

Rod blushed, and Travis found it adorable. It made him want to kiss him. There was no reason he couldn't and every reason to do it. Decision made.

Travis crossed to where Rod was standing in front of the window. As much as he wanted to press him up against the wall and kiss him senseless, Travis restrained himself. Instead he stroked Rod's cheek with one hand before leaning in and pressing his lips softly against Rod's.

The low half sigh, half groan was all Travis needed to continue. He'd been good, waited, slept out on the couch because he knew himself: sleep would not hold him back from needing Rod. "Put your arms around my neck," he whispered against the lips he'd been fantasizing about.

The crutches clattered to the floor as Rod let go and wrapped his arms around Travis's neck. Rod wasn't a small man, but Travis was bigger. Lifting Rod, he walked them both to the couch before releasing his hold to let Rod slip onto the cushions.

Instead of sitting down, Rod tightened his grip on Travis, wrapping his good leg around him. "Bedroom."

"Bedroom?" Please, please, let him not have misheard. At the same time, his stomach clenched with nerves.

"We are going to have sex, right? The bedroom is both of ours?"

Travis tried not to overthink as he carried Rod into their bedroom. He hadn't gone this long without sex in years, but he would wait as long as Rod needed; he didn't want to hurt him, but—Jesus, his brain was freezing up. If someone asked him up or down he would have gotten the answer wrong.

"Quit thinking. Trust me. I asked Dana, she said it was okay."

Travis let Rod slip out of his hands, stepping back for a second to get a clear look at his handsome face.

"Come here," Rod demanded.

He went.

## 17

F inally.

Rod's body was practically vibrating. He suppressed a chuckle as Travis manhandled him into the bedroom. Whatever problem his brain was having, *had*, his body was on board. He was done with this cat-and-mouse game of bed vs. couch.

Travis released his hold. Rod slipped down the front of Travis's body, trying to keep contact for as long as possible, to sit on the edge of the bed. Leaning back on his hands, he allowed himself to enjoy this view of Travis, long and lean—so sexy— worn Levi's low on his hips and a ratty long-sleeve T-shirt. He looked uncharacteristically shy. Rod felt a wicked grin spread across his own face.

Travis stuck his hands in his back pockets. "How're we going to do this?" he asked. "Um, can we, it—I—I want to do this right." He blushed bright red.

Rod let out a little laugh. Travis really was nervous about this. "I'm sure you have an idea of how this works. Come on, can't this be just a little romantic? Do we have to have a military precision operation?"

Travis laughed. It broke some of the tension between them, which Rod was grateful for. He patted the comforter cover next to him. Instead of sitting, Travis scuffed his toe against the carpet.

"Yeah, but this is a big deal, and I don't want to hurt you, and I spent the last two weeks sleeping on the couch dreaming of this moment, and now I am scared as shit. What if I'm terrible, what if it doesn't work between us, what if that Theo guy is the better man for you? You're my best friend; I don't want anything to change—but once we do this, everything will change. Up until now we could turn back, forget what we've done so far." Travis snapped his mouth shut, looking startled that he'd blurted that much out.

Travis, the king of "Hold my beer, watch this." It shocked Rod to hear Travis say he was scared. Rod was scared—nervous as hell—but Travis was never scared. Travis never looked; he always leapt. He was the first to use the rope swing, the first to see if the salsa was as hot as advertised. It was unfathomable to Rod that this moment was something he would balk at. But maybe, a little voice whispered, it was because it really did mean *that* much. He patted the bed next to him again. "Sit next to me."

This time Travis obeyed.

"You still have your shoes on," Rod pointed out.

Grinning sheepishly, Travis leaned down and tugged on his laces before toeing the boots off. They fell to the floor with a clunk. He sat back up, still looking shy and apprehensive.

"Let's turn on a movie. Come on, scoot over here."

"Okay."

Watching TV was familiar ground, something they'd always done together, and Rod had the beginnings of a plan.

They maneuvered around so they were both propped up against the phalanx of pillows Travis had purchased to help make Rod comfortable while he recovered. Rod grabbed the remote from his bedside table and clicked on the TV. He flicked through the movie menu and picked one they'd both seen before.

The current between them was still there, humming beneath the surface as they watched the actors run around trying to save the world from impending doom.

Rod scooted closer to Travis so their hips and shoulders were touching. Travis turned his attention from the screen, putting his arm over Rod's shoulders and tucking him close before turning back to the movie. Rod could tell he wasn't really paying attention. They'd seen this one at least ten times, anyway. Travis's gaze kept flicking sideways. The soundtrack rumbled, and the TV was loud enough to rattle the walls, but Rod felt like he was in the middle of a romcom, not a disaster film where actors were dying right and left.

Travis still just sat there with his arm over Rod's shoulder.

"We've kissed already."

"I know." Travis didn't move, eyes intent on the screen.

"Kiss me again. Those little pecks you've been handing out since then don't count." Travis continued to focus on the TV. Rod was going to rip the damn cord out of the wall. When he was healed, Travis was going to pay.

The TV screen flashed with explosions, and the entire city of Las Angeles went up in flames. Rod leaned closer and nibbled on the shell of Travis's ear. He got the reaction he wanted, because Travis turned his head and Rod was able to kiss him, and this time Travis didn't go back to watching LA burn.

They moaned in unison, and whatever had been holding them back snapped, a thunderstorm after a day of unrelenting humidity and cloud cover. If he could, Rod would have thrown himself over Travis. Kissing Travis like this was everything he had ever imagined and more.

Rod wanted to taste all of Travis, he wanted to crawl in his pocket, he wanted him naked. As they kissed, the arousal he'd been keeping at a simmer for weeks—years—returned in full force. He was painfully hard. Travis's tongue dipped into his mouth, licking and tasting, and Rod caught it and sucked hard.

Travis bucked against him and pulled back. "Jesus, Rod," he whispered, wonder and lust warring in his bright blue eyes.

"Take your clothes off."

Travis started to say something.

Rod cut him off. "Now." Damn, he couldn't wait until he was fully healed. He stripped his own shirt off, dropping it on the floor, then twisted around to pull off his cotton sweat-shorts, as well as his soft cast. The ripping Velcro sound stopped Travis in his tracks.

"What are you doing?"

"Dude, there is a piece of metal in there keeping the whole shebang in place. The stitches are healed; I am practically the Six Million Dollar Man. As long as we are careful, like no hand-stands, I'll be fine."

"What if *I* did a handstand?" Travis asked as he slid his jeans down, revealing what Rod had suspected: he was commando.

Rod stopped arguing, the sight of Travis naked and aroused almost too much. Instead he contemplated the image of himself on his back while Travis lowered himself down from a hand-stand to kiss him. "Yes, please, but can we just... get on with it?" He flopped back onto the bed.

"Who's all bossy now? You think this is how this is going to work?" Travis teased. He tumbled onto the bed, naked and glori-ous. It seemed like he'd shed whatever reservations he'd harbored along with his clothes.

"I'm not bossy, I'm horny. I want you to make me come, and then I want to do it again, because I'm not going to last long enough the first time."

"Oh yeah?" Instead of grabbing him, Travis stilled, his

expression changing to one Rod had never seen on him before. He looked... predatory.

Shit.

"You just lie there sexy as fuck, and I'll make you forget everything—including coming before I tell you to."

Shit. Shit. Shit. Rod trembled.

"Put your hands over your head."

"I want to touch you."

"Yeah." Travis's slow smile was as wicked as anything Rod had ever seen. "I want that too, but if you do I'm gonna forget what else I want to do, so put your hands over your head."

He put his hands over his head.

Travis reached out to run a hand down Rod's face, chest, and abs, stopping before he reached Rod's dick. Rod let out a soft sigh. He knew it was going to happen, but the anticipation was driving him to the edge of too much. Travis followed the path of his hand with his mouth, kissing Rod quickly on the lips, the chin, his collarbone. He licked a nipple and drew a wet path with his tongue. Rod felt himself pulse, and even though he couldn't see it, he knew he was leaking precome onto his belly.

"You are so sexy."

"Yeah, so sexy with a gimp leg covered with scars."

"Yes," was all Travis said before he continued exploring, and Rod had to close his eyes. He lost himself in the sensation of Travis's hands and tongue learning his body. The juxtaposition of his rough, callused palms and his mouth—soft lips, sharp teeth—it was all too good. Rod didn't need much. It had been so long since anything other than his own hand had pleasured him.

"I can't..." Whatever he was going to say died away as Travis moved back up and licked Rod from his heavy sac to the tip of his shaft. He pulsed again, and Travis licked again.

"You're gonna to make me come." Rod opened his eyes to watch him; he couldn't help it.

Travis gripped him tightly around the base of his cock. "Don't."

"Fuck, me," he ground out.

"Yeah, that's what I want. I want to fuck you. I want to feel you around me and I want to come so deep inside you…"

"Please." Rod had never begged for anything in his life, but he was willing to beg for this. "I'm not going to break. It's my leg, not my ass, and all we need are a ton of pillows—amazingly, we have like seventy here on the bed—and me on my side."

"Let me suck you a little while first. I want to taste you too."

"Jesus fucking Christ."

Travis moved downward, taking him as far into his throat as he could in one move. Rod had to force himself to listen to the terrible dialogue coming from the TV in order to not shoot into his mouth. Travis's blond head bobbed up and down as he licked, sucked, and nibbled up and down Rod's shaft. It was only sheer force of will that kept Rod from releasing. He was letting out involuntary grunts and groans as he tried to control himself. Trav let go of the base of Rod's cock, instead holding his sac in an almost painful grip. The need to come receded just enough, and Rod still held his arms above his pillow.

Trav raised his head. "You are very, very good. I can't believe we waited this long."

"It wasn't because I wanted to, believe me," Rod muttered.

"Yeah, I know. I'm gonna make up for it."

"Not if you kill me through lack of orgasm." He broke form, grabbing the back of Travis's head and a handful of blond hair and dragging him up for a kiss. "I can't believe I get to do this," Rod said when they came up for air.

"Yeah." Trav stroked his face again. Rod felt Trav's erection bump against his thigh. Without any further hesitation, Trav tucked pillows under Rod's leg and plastered himself against his back.

"Tell me we have lube."

Rod felt Travis's smile and knew the answer.

Soon those callused fingers slipped between his thighs and made their way to his hole, stopping to caress his balls again before massaging his entrance. Rod liked ass play as much as the next guy, but he was done with foreplay. Until Trav pushed his finger all the way inside, making him take a breath. He loved the feel of the stretch around another man's—Travis's—fingers. He added another one, and Rod bore down to take them in.

"Fuck, Rod, you are incredible," Travis breathed into his ear. "I don't want to stop."

"Please don't."

Travis found his prostate about then and rendered Rod speechless, pinned against Travis and unable to do anything but reel in the sensations, in the ever-growing reality that he was going to come and Travis wouldn't be able to stop it this time.

Travis pulled his fingers out.

There was a *snick*, and then Travis was back, his fingers slick and chilly, pushing lube inside and coating his own cock. Finally Rod felt it, the head of Travis's cock against him, and he almost came from that except for the initial discomfort as his body remembered what it was like to have over half a foot of cock up inside him.

Trav pulled Rod's thigh so he was half lying on Travis, half on his side, forcing Trav's cock even further in, way up and against his prostate. Rod let Travis take the lead, helping their bodies move together. Travis wrapped a hand around Rod's dripping erection. Rod watched as Travis gripped him tightly, feeling the way the soft outer skin of his cock slid over his hardness.

This time he wouldn't be able to stop. Precome was oozing out; his balls were so full and tight... Travis muttered something in his ear, then bit the sensitive lobe. Rod moaned and grabbed the hand Travis had on his cock, helping him push down harder and tighter as he clenched around Travis and came, the fluid dripping over their joined hands. He felt it as Travis orgasmed too, the heat of it flooding him and making his body try to come a little more. Travis collapsed half under him, his arm still wrapped around Rod's waist, hand on his slowly shrinking erection.

Rod wanted to stay in that cocoon forever. It was perfect. He and Travis together was perfect; it was more than perfect.

Travis muttered, "That was fucking incredible."

"Yeah, that."

Travis eased away, and Rod pouted because he missed him already.

"I'm grabbing a washcloth."

Rod rolled onto his back. When Travis returned from the bathroom, he gently wiped Rod down and crawled onto the bed next to him, pulling the cover around them.

"Those pillowcases are going to need a wash."

"Not this minute. Besides, we might need them again."

Rod's dick twitched at the thought, but then his stomach growled in protest. He debated for a minute: food or sex? Travis tucked up against Rod, his skin cool from being out of bed, and Rod forgot about his stomach. Who needed food anyway?

———————

## 18

Travis woke in stages. Slowly he became aware that he wasn't sleeping on the couch and that the weight of Rod's body was pressing him into the mattress they were sharing. He smiled as the memory of what they had done the night before came flooding back. Having sex with Rod was much, much better than he had imagined. And he'd thought he was very creative.

"What're you smiling about?"

He opened his eyes and met Rod's sleepy gaze. He still hadn't gotten a haircut. Curls were starting to form, and a few strands were sticking straight up, sexy as fuck. "I'm pretty sure you know exactly what I'm smiling about."

"Yeah? Hmm, maybe I need a reminder?" Rod rolled on top of Travis, grinding his morning erection into Travis's answering one.

"Don't you have a date with Gloria?"

"I'll catch up. I'm faster than her now." Rod stuck his tongue out and licked along Travis's lips, then gently nipped at his bottom lip before moving to his ear. "Besides, I think we have a lot of make-up sex to take care of."

"We were never fighting." Travis was perplexed.

"No, but it took us way too long to get here, in this bed. We have a lot of sexy-time to make up for."

"Hmm. I don't really have an argument against that." Travis carefully rolled Rod off him and onto his side, their erections bumping against each other. "But I'm not doing anything that will push back your recovery." Without waiting for an answer, Travis pulled Rod's thigh up so it was supported by Travis's body, "I'll drive. You hold on."

He grasped their cocks in one fist, glad for his big hands. Rod held Travis's face between his palms, devouring his mouth. Between the sensation of their cocks rubbing against each other, slick and hard, and Rod's tongue either halfway down his throat in an attempt to swallow Travis whole or licking and sucking along the top of his mouth and lips, Travis knew he wasn't going to last. Funny how even though he controlled the stick it felt like Rod was at the wheel.

He changed his grip a little, letting the tip of his thumb rub up against the soft underside of their cocks. Rod moaned. Travis did it again, and once more, both of them thrusting now. Rod broke off the kiss, dropping his head against Travis's shoulder. Seconds later, Travis felt Rod shudder, and warm come pulsed across his hand, pushing him all the way to orgasm.

"Fuck me." Rod rolled onto his back, staring at the ceiling.

"I will, baby, I will."

A FEW DAYS LATER, Travis dropped Rod off at the mall ten minutes late because they'd lost track of time. Travis was still on a high from the blow job Rod had given him—and of course he'd had to reciprocate. The soft cast on Rod's leg was coming off soon, but the walks with Gloria were a welcome habit and gave Travis time to keep exploring his options in

Skagit. They'd talked a little about the future, but Travis still sensed a kernel of doubt from his lover. He had a couple hours and an idea he wanted to investigate before picking Rod up, and then they were going to visit Jasper that evening. Not enough time to figure everything out, but enough for an outline.

Rod turned and waved. As he made his way inside, Travis could see several other figures inside already and figured Rod was about to get a talking-to from his friend.

He hadn't told Rod, but after more than a month of silence he'd gotten a series of disturbing texts from his mother hinting that the long-threatened trip to Skagit to "talk some sense into" him was now imminent. He hadn't talked to her since he left, as his dad had insisted he had everything under control. Travis didn't have a clear idea of what was happening between his parents, but his dad had asked him please not to worry about that, to take care of Rod and keep researching options in Skagit. He was doing that. Taking care of Rod was second nature.

Travis worried anyway: about his dad, about the farm, about everyone's future... about people he felt he'd let down. He couldn't figure out how to fix things. He'd said as much to his dad only the night before.

"Son, you are not the problem. You are working on finding a solution that works for you and Rod. We will figure out the farm; who knows, maybe Abigail will want to be a part of it. Or maybe when the time comes for me to retire, we'll sell. Don't worry. We'll get through this, one way or another. As far as the business right now goes, I've got all the help I need. All those people we pay actually do work, you know." His dad chuckled, and he was right; they had a lot of help, seasonal and otherwise, who loved working for Walker Enterprises.

"Fine, fine."

Travis *had* to be satisfied with that for now. He could only move forward, not back, and besides, he *wanted* to be where he was now, not miserable and stupid like he'd been before.

After watching Rod enter the mall—under his own power these days, no crutches—he directed his truck toward the farmers market he'd heard so much about. The real estate agent he'd been talking to had mentioned it as well. Travis figured a farmer was a farmer; he'd see what the market had to offer.

He was impressed. The market was much larger than he'd expected, extending the length of several city blocks in downtown Skagit. About half the market was covered and seemingly permanent, while the other half set up under the open sky. Today they were lucky: it was beautiful, only a few clouds in the spring sky and not a chance of rain.

The market offered something for everyone: spring veggies and fresh-cut flowers, handmade sausages and deli meats, fresh-baked breads and pastries, even essential oils. An older gentleman sold thunder gourds, whatever those were. And it was packed with people; many of the stalls had lines of customers waiting their turn. The sausage stall had "Sold Out" signs covering several of their offerings.

"Travis?" a familiar voice called over the din of the crowd.

Travis turned to see Cam waving at him from a few stalls down. Waving back, he wove through the crowd to where Cam stood in front of the largest display of produce Travis had seen yet.

"Cam, how's it going? Where's Ira?" The two of them were usually together unless Cam was bartending. Although Travis remembered that Cam had told him he was applying to the local university for fall-term classes.

"Good. Ira's painting and getting ready for a show in LA. Travis, this is a good friend of mine, Brandon Campbell. He and his wife are big organic farmers; they're huge providers to local restaurants, and there's even Seattle places on his list."

Travis leaned across the colorful root vegetables, swiss chard, lettuces—the rest he had no idea of—to shake Brandon's hand. Brandon was incredibly handsome, Travis couldn't help but notice. An enormous shaggy black dog stood up and ambled over, standing next to Travis so that his head was under Travis's hand. A not-so-subtle request for a scratch on the head. Travis complied.

"Don't mind him, he's just nosy. Sit back down, Pronto." Pronto let out a big dog sigh and returned to the back of the booth where he'd been sitting. Travis had always wanted a dog, but Lenore said they were too much work and the house would be full of hair. Travis thought vacuuming was a small price to pay for companionship. He wondered if Rod might want a dog. They could start with a dog and work up to a kid. Maybe. The idea of kids scared Travis, but not as much as it once had. He was pretty sure that had to do with being with the right person.

"Travis is from eastern Washington; he's some kind of farmer too," Cam added to his introduction.

"Oh? They've got a lot of grapes out there," Brandon said.

"I grow wheat. But grapes are something I've been thinking about." A few weeks earlier when he'd been talking to his dad on the phone, Michael had mentioned that there was a vineyard going in a few miles from them. And while Travis didn't want to live in Walla Walla anymore, he wondered if he and his dad could use his little patch of earth for grapes. Every time he went to the grocery store he marveled at the wine selection, especially the successful boutique wineries from east of the Cascades. He'd spent hours doing research.

He and Brandon fell into a long discussion about terroir, soil, and crop variety. About long winters, summers, and the economics of farming. It wasn't often Travis met someone close to his age who was excited about farming and actually knew what they were doing. For Travis it had always been a chore, one he was expected to do for his entire life—at least until recently.

"I've experimented with grapes out here, but we really don't get enough sunshine," Brandon said. "The area is good for the German and Swiss wine grape varietals, but that's a smaller market. Have you thought seriously about grapes?"

Almost like when he fully understood what Rod meant to him, that he loved him, Travis knew he was on the right track—something he could do in Skagit and probably love, the missing piece in his plan. Grapes, grapes, grapes. He couldn't wait to talk to his dad again.

He and Brandon exchanged cell numbers.

Cam had stayed, patiently listening to their conversation. "I don't think I've ever seen two people that excited about dirt."

"Shut up, you, dirt is cool."


A MAROON SEDAN he didn't recognize was parked facing the wrong direction in front of their house when Travis pulled into the driveway after picking Rod up at the mall. They'd also taken Gloria to her assisted living facility and stopped to spend time with Jasper, which was fun but also kind of exhausting. Travis was looking forward to an evening of bad TV. After setting the brake, he peered over at the car.

"Crap."

"What?" Rod asked as he twisted to look out Travis's window.

Travis knew the profile of the person sitting in the passenger seat; he would recognize her anywhere. It was his mother. At one time he would have welcomed her. It had been over six weeks since he'd seen her last; he would've invited her inside his new home and hoped they could come to an understanding. From where he sat now, she looked angry and bitter. There was someone in the driver's seat, but Travis couldn't see who it was. "It's Lenore," he said.

"What's she doing here?" Rod peered over at the car. "And who is with her?"

"I can only imagine that it's not good—and, who knows? You go in the house; I'll take care of this."

They'd talked about what Lenore had done in the past and how she was reacting now. Travis didn't want Rod to worry about it.

"Look, nothing she has to say is going to change my mind," he repeated, in case Rod had forgotten their conversations.

"I'm not worried about you changing your mind. But you're not facing her by yourself. We're a team now. Partners. Get it?" Rod opened the door of the truck and hopped out, not waiting for Travis to reply, and started to limp toward the car.

Travis quickly followed, watching as his mom and then Lisa Harris, of all people, emerged from the small car. He and Rod stopped and stared. What the hell was Lisa doing here? Last Travis knew, they'd agreed to act like the engagement had never happened. He hadn't heard from her since she left on the trip with her dad, and he'd figured he would never talk to her again.

He looked at his mother with eyes wide open. No longer through the lens of a boy who thought she could do no wrong. Travis thought about what Abigail had told him about how Lenore had treated her growing up, and he wondered why a person would choose to give their love conditionally the way his mother had. He shook his head; there was no good answer to that question.

"Mom, what are you doing here?" he called out as he started making his way toward her.

Lenore came around the front of the car to meet him. It was then he saw a small pistol in her hand. He froze; his mother was a great shot and knew her way around weapons. The two of them had spent hours together at the shooting range when he was a kid.

"What, you aren't even going to say hello to your mother? Do I not deserve a hug anymore? Instead you threw your life away to be with a faggot?"

His stomach sunk further at her words. She was not the person he remembered from childhood at all. She was an angry, homophobic person who couldn't bring herself to love her own son if he chose to love another man. "Mom, why do you have a gun? Lisa, what's going on?"

Looking closer at Lisa, he could see she was barely keeping herself under control; her face was tight with strain and exhaustion.

"Don't speak." Lenore waved the gun between the three of them.

Travis was terrified. Not for himself; if his time was today it was today, but he guessed his mother wouldn't shoot him. She had someone else in mind. If she believed Travis was going to stand there and let her shoot Rod, she was—well, she'd crossed the line into irrational, and Travis didn't know how to help her anymore. Maybe he never had.

"Hi, Lisa," Rod said, not acknowledging Lenore or her gun.

They were standing in broad daylight on the front lawn of their new house. The house and city they were making their new life in. This was not happening. Travis tried to think what he could do to defuse this suddenly intense situation.

Rod kept his attention on Lisa. "You must be thirsty after the long drive; would you like to come inside? Travis went grocery shopping yesterday. I'm pretty sure there's food in the house."

Lisa began to move toward Rod, something like relief crossing her face.

"You're already turning Travis into a woman," Lenore hissed. "Homosexual."

"Mom," Travis implored. He needed to get them off the front lawn, away from innocent bystanders who happened to drive or walk past. Lenore was a good shot, but the way she was acting right now, Travis doubted if she was really in control. He didn't want her taking any kind of shot; anyone could get caught in the line of fire the way she was waving the gun around. "Does Dad know you're here?"

"He went to the Tri-Cities," she said by way of answer, which probably meant he didn't know. "You're grocery shopping for the faggot now?" she continued. "Does he have you scrubbing the kitchen floor too? Making breakfast and dinner, taking care of the laundry. Are you the *woman* now, Travis?" Lenore screamed those last words like being a woman was the worst thing she could think of.

"We're partners, Mom, we do everything together. I'm sure you've noticed there is no woman in our relationship. We are two men who love each other and—"

"Shut your mouth. Shut up. Just *shut up*," she screamed, waving the gun around again. It was almost five o'clock in the evening; some of their neighbors were home or arriving home. Travis saw a curtain twitch in the window across the street. They hadn't met many of the neighbors yet, and somehow his mom shooting one of them seemed like a bad way to begin.

"Mom, can we take this inside? Please?"

In the distance he heard a faint siren. He wondered if someone had already called the police or if SkPD was responding to something else. Rod and Lisa both remained standing between the house and the car. It must have been a rental car, or maybe it was Lisa's. Travis didn't know.

His mom heard the siren too, and he heard the safety click off. His attention was divided between Rod and Lisa, his mother, and the figure coming up behind his mother on the sidewalk. With car doors opening and closing around the neighborhood and traffic sounds from the larger arterial two blocks over, plus being completely focused on the three of them, Lenore had no idea anyone was behind her.

A man wearing a dark suit and tie had quietly crossed the street. Travis had watched out of the corner of his eye as the man left his house to approach Lenore from behind. All of them—Travis, Rod, and Lisa—could see him, but no one gave any indication. Travis wanted to warn him off, but something about the way he moved had Travis thinking he was a professional. He moved with catlike grace; for as bulky a guy as he was, he approached unseen and unheard.

"Mom, why are you doing this?" He only needed to keep her talking and focused on him for a few more seconds. A minute at most.

"Why am I doing this?" She threw the words back at him in disgust. "Why? You dare to ask me why?"

"Yes, why? Why is it more important to you for me to be with a woman than with the person who makes me happiest in the entire world? I don't understand."

"Don't say that in front of your fiancée." She waved the gun toward Lisa. Travis realized that was probably how Lenore had gotten Lisa to drive all the way from Walla Walla.

"Lisa and I broke it off months ago, Mom. We aren't engaged; we aren't getting married. There is nothing between us."

"I tried to tell her." Lisa spoke for the first time. She'd edged closer to Rod. They were only a few feet apart and much closer to the front door than they had been.

Lenore saw the direction of his gaze and turned her focus to Rod. "You should have died in that accident; it would have saved a lot of trouble. Things would be right. I would be on my way to having a grandchild." Travis's heart clenched at her words, at her disregard of their lives and happiness.

The suited man grabbed Lenore from behind in a wrestling

hold and knocked the gun from her hand in one swift movement. His mother screamed and cursed as the big man wrestled her to the ground and held her down with a knee in her back. He was twice her size, but Lenore was screaming obscenities and thrashing around trying to get loose. Travis went to her, not knowing what else to do.

"Mom, stop struggling. Please."

She spat at him, a huge globule nearly landing on his boot. Travis was so shocked he almost let it hit him.

A police cruiser sped around the corner and screeched to a stop behind Lisa's car. Two uniformed SkPD officers got out, hurrying over to where the stranger was holding down his mother.

One of the officers cuffed Lenore while the other called in that they'd arrived and the disturbance had been contained.

The stranger stood up and brushed off his suit before holding out a hand to Travis.

"Adam Klay, I live across the street." He pointed at the house he'd come out of, the older two-story home kitty-corner from them with a large front porch and an even larger maple tree in the front yard.

Travis shook Adam's hand, his own hand shaking a little.

"Thank you." He felt a hand against the small of his back. From the touch alone he knew it was Rod. He leaned into the comfort, the adrenaline leaking out of him, leaving him shaking and weak.

"What happened?" Adam asked, motioning for them to step away from where Lenore was lying. One of the officers bent to help her to her feet, and she started yelling again.

"I don't know where to start. But I guess the short story is that that's my mother, and she objects to me and Rod being together." And now she'd helped out them to the entire neighborhood. There was not hiding your sexuality, and then there was announcing to everyone within earshot what you did in the bedroom.

"Hi, I'm Rod, Travis's partner. And you are?" Travis smirked a little Rod's possessiveness, at the same time that he reveled in it.

"Adam Klay, neighbor and," he reached into his suit jacket to pull out a leather wallet and flipped it open to reveal a shiny badge, "FBI." He slipped the badge back into his jacket pocket.

"You live across the street? We have an FBI agent living across the street?" Rod shook his head, "Uh, sorry—anyway, to answer your question, from what Lisa's said and I've pieced together, Travis's mom forced Lisa to drive across the state at gunpoint so she could confront him about being in a relationship with me."

One of the uniformed officers spoke up. "Looks like this one is ours, Klay. We'll take over from here. Thanks for the assist."

Adam shook hands with Travis and Rod again. "Hell of a welcome to the neighborhood. If you're up for it, come knock on our door. I'm sure my boyfriend would love to meet you. If it's warm enough, we'll sit out back." With that he strode back across the street to his house.

Boyfriend?

The officer was watching them and chuckled at their stunned expressions. "Klay's a good guy. You're lucky he was here. I'm going to need to ask you a few questions and take down your statements. Do you want to go inside?"

Travis knew Rod had to be tired from standing as long as they had, and he figured they could all use a coffee or something.

"Yeah. Let's do this inside." He held a hand out to Lisa, who'd joined them, and together they went inside. Rod was the one who noticed she was shaking and found a blanket to wrap around her shoulders.

"We meet again. I didn't think it would be like this," Travis heard him say.

"You're telling me. She asked me to stop by and then said she needed a ride. I thought she was acting weird. We hadn't talked since Travis and I called it off, but I was trying to be a better person. Serves me right. I'm going back to carrying pepper spray."

"Pepper spray?"

Travis groaned and took himself into the kitchen to start a pot of coffee.

"He didn't tell you? The night he broke it off, I kind of lost it and ran after him with my self-defense spray. Lucky for him he's fast."

Travis heard Rod try to keep himself from laughing. He supposed it was good they could find something funny in all this.

"Don't get any ideas!" he yelled.

It must have been the come-down from all the adrenaline, because there really was nothing funny about being pepper sprayed, but Lisa started to laugh, which set off a chain reaction, and soon all three of them were laughing so hard they were crying. One of the officers poked his head through the open door. "Everybody okay?"

They assured him they were. Travis found cups and poured them all coffee, then went to sit on the couch with Rod.

One of the police officers took his mother away in an ambulance. She would be held in a psychiatric ward for evaluation, he said. When Travis called his dad to let him know what had happened, he started shaking and felt something a lot like tears pressing from behind his eyes. Again, Rod was right there, rubbing his back while he talked.

"I'm on my way, son. I'm so sorry." His dad had answered immediately, and by the time Travis was halfway through his story he could hear the sound of tires on asphalt competing with Michael's voice as he drove. "I'm taking the back way. I'll be there as soon as I can. I should have seen something like this coming." His dad sounded sad and a little broken. Travis didn't know what to say.

"I love you, Dad."

"I love you too, son."

The remaining officer quickly and professionally took their statements, taking longest with Lisa. When he was finished, he flipped his notebook shut, and Travis showed him to the door.

"There may be more questions; we'll be in touch."

"Thanks for all your help."

"Protect and serve." He winked at Travis. First the FBI and then the cop? Travis was liking Skagit better and better.

AFTER GIVING HER STATEMENT, Lisa borrowed Travis's phone—Lenore had made her throw hers out the car window—and called her dad to reassure him she would be okay, but no, she wasn't coming home that night.

"You can stay here; we have a spare room." Rod spoke before Travis could. "I mean, if you're okay with that. It seems horrible to have to pay for a hotel room—although we could pay for one if you'd prefer not to be here."

Lisa cocked her head, clearly thinking about Rod's offer. She wrapped her arms protectively around herself. "Yes, I'll stay, thank you for the offer. I don't think I want to be alone tonight, even in a hotel with other people. I mean—I'm okay. I never believed she'd really hurt me, but I was afraid she'd cause an accident. It's all been... a lot."

"God, I am so sorry." Travis couldn't believe his own mother abducted his ex-fiancée at gunpoint. Some things just couldn't be made up.

"Thank you. Travis, I know you're not to blame. It was a little bit of a come-to-Jesus moment when she pulled that gun out, I'm not going to lie."

He rolled his eyes. "I'm kind of to blame." Rod squeezed his arm.

She cocked her head, pinning him with a surprisingly sympathetic gaze. "Not really. I'm a small-town girl, but I've been around. I've read books; I did leave for college. I don't live under a rock. I've thought a lot about life since we called off the engagement. My dad and I had time to talk on our trip. The terrible things Lenore said about you and Rod and women in general—she put my feelings in perspective. You did hurt me, but you tried to do the right thing, which I appreciate more now. Lenore has a serious case of internalized misogyny."

"I'm sorry for everything."

"Travis, I could have been like her, I think. You and I weren't meant to be together. I know you're sorry, and like I said, it's not your fault. Anyway, I know it's only seven, but I need to take a shower and go to bed."

Travis showed her the bathroom and the spare bedroom.

"There are fresh towels under the sink. And I could loan you a T-shirt or something to sleep in."

"I'm good, thanks."



TRAVIS WAS WONDERING when the press would come knocking at their door, but then Rod pointed out that Adam Klay was a federal agent and wondered if there had been some sort of media blackout so they wouldn't be bothered. If so, Travis was grateful. One day they would take Adam up on his offer to meet his partner and drink wine on the patio. Not this night. "What a weird day."

"That's an understatement. Let's watch a movie until your dad gets here."

"Does 'a movie' mean sex?" Travis asked hopefully.

"Travis, your ex-fiancée is sleeping in the room across the hall."

"We could turn up the volume?"

"No," Rod said firmly. "How about you get on the phone and order pizza? Get a loaded one; I'm starving. Ask Lisa what she wants."

Travis's stomach rumbled in agreement. Rod grinned. Damn, Travis was glad to know that grin was all his.

Lisa didn't want anything, but Travis and Rod scarfed down most of the large pizza in under ten minutes. Maybe not a record —they weren't eighteen anymore—but close.


In their bedroom Rod stripped down to nothing, including taking his cast off, and crawled under the sheets.

"You need anything? Water? A beer?" Travis asked.

"I just need you to get in bed and hold me."

"I can do that."

Rod watched, grinning while Travis stripped, then snuggled next to him under the covers. Travis draped an arm across Rod's chest and pressed his nose into the base of Rod's neck, breathing a sigh of... something. Relief? Relaxation? Rod must've felt it too.

"I'm sorry about your mom," Rod whispered into the quiet of the room.

"I am too." He was sorry. Sorry that she had turned a corner somewhere that had led to a place of such hatred. Sorry for his dad and his sister. Had his mom put aside dreams to marry Michael? She'd never talked about anything other than their family and the farm. Had she wanted to be something different but instead ended up stuck forever in a place from which she felt she couldn't escape? How was his dad going to cope?

There wasn't much to say. It was impossible for Travis to know what Michael would do. In the past weeks he had stood by Travis's side and supported him, but Travis didn't know how this incident would affect him.

"Wanna watch *Volcano*?" Rod asked.

"I suppose." Travis lifted his head so Rod could witness the terrible pout. "If we can't have sex, I'll settle for a hot and sweaty Tommy Lee Jones."

Rod clicked the TV on, and the sounds of LA imploding under the heat of a volcano filled the room.

"She'll think we're having sex anyway if it's this loud," Travis said. "We might as well."

## 19

I gnoring Rod's halfhearted protest, Travis snaked a hand across his abdomen and began stroking him. Rod shut his eyes, attempting to stifle a groan. His traitorous cock hardened under Travis's caresses and, worse, he'd apparently used up his spine for the day. He bucked into Trav's grip, reveling in the sensation against his better judgment.

"We'll just do this," Travis whispered into Rod's ear. He pushed against Rod's hip, turning him onto his side, and molded himself to Rod's back, his erection pressing insistently into the crack of Rod's ass.

As LA burned and Tommy Lee bossed people around, Trav kept his grip on Rod steady and firm, rutting against his back, his erection slipping between Rod's ass cheeks to nudge against his hole, teasing. Rod wanted nothing more than to feel Travis shoot against him, the heat of come and reassurance of life. He pushed back against Travis and could feel Travis's chest rising and falling with the exertion. Back and forth—into Travis's hand, against Travis's groin—they set a rhythm that was easy and slick. Precome oozed from his slit, giving Travis a little lube.

Travis rubbed his thumb along the top, pressing into the soft head of his shaft.

"Trav..."

"Yeah, I've got you. I've always got you."

Travis thrust again against Rod's back. Rod twisted his torso, needing Travis's lips against his own, needing to have his mouth on Travis somewhere, anywhere. The kiss wasn't gentle; it was a clashing of teeth and sucking and gnawing, and it ended with Travis groaning into his mouth as he shuddered against Rod, hot and slick.

"Fuck..."

One more twist of Travis's grip was all it took for Rod to follow him over the edge. He stuffed a fist into his mouth to keep their guest from hearing his release.

Some time later—Rod only knew it was fully dark outside— he felt Travis roll out of bed and fumble around for clothing.

"What's up?" Rod whispered.

"My dad's here—well, at the hospital. I'm going to meet him."

"You want me to come?"

"Not this time. Tomorrow, maybe. I know he wants to see you." Travis leaned down to drop a kiss on his forehead before leaving the room. Rod drifted in and out of sleep, but it was restless. It wasn't until Travis returned to bed several hours later, in the early hours of the morning, that he was able to fall completely back to sleep.

"They're what?" Travis asked sleepily.

Rod felt terrible waking Travis after he'd come back so late from meeting Michael. He wanted to stay in their bed and hold Travis close. It didn't matter that it had been hours since Lenore had held the gun on them; Rod had seen their life together flash before his eyes.

"What?" Travis repeated, bleary and not awake.

Rod watched Travis visibly try to shake off his sleep fog. Despite how guilty Rod felt, Travis was adorable when he was half asleep. His sleep habits hadn't changed much since they were kids: the fitted sheet was half pulled off his side of the bed, the blanket was discarded on the floor, and he had one pillow under his head while most of the others were also on the floor. Unlike their childhood sleepovers, Rod had fallen asleep with Travis's arm possessively holding him around the middle. He'd woken up mostly the same way, except for the tornado of bedding.

Rod had been using Travis as a pillow when the buzz of his phone on the nightstand had caught his attention. He'd been expecting a daily news roundup or something, not a text from his dad.

"My dad and Meg are on their way. I got a text that was a picture of the Space Needle!" He checked his phone again. "It came like an hour ago. They'll be here any minute."

The words seemed to finally sink in. Travis sat up. The remaining bit of sheet pooled in his lap, but it didn't hide anything. Slowly, he slipped out from under the blanket to stand in front of Rod.

A naked Travis was more distraction than Rod could deal with. Grabbing his hand, Rod attempted to propel Travis toward the shower.

"Why are we in a hurry?" Travis blinked slowly.

Okay, so maybe he wasn't as awake as Rod had hoped.

"They're on their way! I forgot they were coming! You have to admit a lot has been going on. It's not every day your partner's mother kidnaps someone at gunpoint."

That seemed to wake Travis up. His blue eyes were sharp and alert now. "What about Lisa? And my dad's on the couch."

Rod groaned. "I forgot she was here. Shit god damn, get dressed, get in the shower—not in that order. I'll tell Lisa we have company."

Leaving Travis to find clothes, Rod finished pulling on his shorts and cast—he was going to be ecstatic when it finally came off for good—and knocked on Lisa's door. There was no answer, so he went to find her. Michael's eyes opened as he passed through the living room to the kitchen, where he found a note propped against the coffee pot.

"I'm going to take a quick shower, if you two don't mind," Michael said.

"Please, make yourself at home. But you're going to have to hurry to beat Trav."

Michael disappeared down the hallway and into the bathroom.

"She's already left!" Rod called out. Travis shuffled into the living room with no shirt on and his shorts unbuttoned, displaying the beginning of his treasure trail. If it weren't for the elder Walker, and his own dad practically at the front door, Rod would have dragged Travis right back to bed and taken advantage of him.

"Come on, Trav," he urged, "any minute, remember?"

"I'll get dressed, I promise, but I want to feel you again first. You got up too fast." He was pouting.

Rod relented, peeking down the hallway to where the bathroom door remained shut. "Come here."

Suspiciously more alert-looking and wearing a naughty smile, Travis closed the distance between them. His smile deepened further, the blue of his eyes limitless. Rod was willfully ensnared. Travis tipped Rod's chin up just enough so he could lean in and drop a kiss on his lips. Travis may have meant the kiss to be playful, but it was a dead-serious promise.

Travis held Rod's chin and plundered his mouth. Rod opened wide, wanting it all. Travis sucked Rod's tongue into his own mouth, then released him to suck and nibble on his lower lip. Fuck.

"Trav..." Rod tried to speak.

Travis wrapped his arms around Rod, pulling him tight against his own body, and Rod gave up his protest. Who cared if his dad arrived and they had their hands down each other's pants? This was their house. Kissing Travis was like nothing Rod had experienced before. Like everything Travis did, he did it thoroughly and with confidence. It turned Rod on to give Travis control.

It was inevitable that they were still making out like a couple of horny high-schoolers when the knock came on the front door.

"Ungh, just a second," Rod called out, reluctantly pulling away. "You asshole, I have an erection.

"I know." Travis cupped him quickly, squeezing just a little. "So do I." He turned and went back into the bedroom. Rod quickly pulled a sweatshirt Travis had left out over his head, hoping it would drop down far enough to hide the evidence of his arousal. He went to answer the door.

IT HAD BEEN at least five years since Rod had seen his dad in person. The last time had been when he graduated college. It was funny how he was the same and yet somehow different. Rod couldn't put his finger on it at first but then realized his dad looked happy, content. There was amusement in his eyes as he passed Rod and came into the house. It was slightly disquieting to think he had no clear memories of his dad being happy, laughing, while he grew up.

"Hi, Dad." He felt unexpectedly awkward as he stood back to let his dad, Meg, and two as-yet-unidentified teenagers into the house. They all trooped past him into the living room. His dad, at the end of the line, stopped in front of Rod.

"Hi, son." Will grabbed him by the shoulders, looking Rod over before engulfing him in a huge hug. Something else Rod never recalled his father doing before. After the surprise wore off, Rod hugged his dad back. His dad let go, saying, "You look good, Rod. Although the sweatshirt is on backward."

Rod looked down at himself. Sure enough, he'd pulled the sweatshirt on so that the tag was in the front. He groaned at himself and quickly pulled his arms inside it and turned it right way around.

Travis emerged from the bedroom, fully dressed, thank god, although he had stolen one of Rod's shirts instead of putting on his own. Tit for tat.

He looked at the rumpled blanket on the couch. "Where's Dad?"

"Shower. He should be about done, though."

Travis headed for Meg. "Good morning. I'm Travis." He stuck out a hand. Meg chuckled and shook it. "Meg Beton-White, pleased to meet you both." She indicated the teens with a wave. "Morgan and Alex, the terrible two."

Morgan and Alex looked to be somewhere around fifteen, although Rod had no way of knowing. Somewhere along the way he'd lost the ability to tell how old someone was.

"Mom, that joke was never funny."

"If a joke is never funny, is it a joke?" Travis asked.

The two looked at Travis suspiciously. One asked, "Are you trying to *relate* to us?"

Travis looked offended. "No. That's a serious question."

Rod snickered and started to say something, but Meg got there first. "Alex, be polite."

"Dad, can I talk to you for a sec?" Rod led his dad into the kitchen, where he filled him in on the events of the day before.

"How can I help? How can *we* help?"

"I don't know. I don't think there is much else to do. Travis's dad drove in late last night. Travis met him at the hospital and stayed with him for a while. There isn't much Michael can do, either, until they evaluate Lenore. Lisa says she isn't going to press charges, but…"

"Wow."

"I'm glad you're here." As he said the words, Rod realized they were true. He'd felt emotionally tetherless for such a long time, beginning back when his parents were still married to each other. Now people were starting to fill up his life. He was happy.

"I'm glad too. It shouldn't have taken this long. But sometimes humans can be pretty stupid. Let's go make a plan for the day, and we'll get out of your way for now. If you think Travis won't mind, I'd like to at least offer some support to Michael."

"I think he'd appreciate it, and I don't mind," Travis said, poking his head into the kitchen. "We're going to head out, though. We'll meet up with you later if he's up for it." Travis kissed Rod quickly before grabbing his keys from the kitchen counter and heading out the door with his father.

Rod watched them leave and wished he could do something more to help the Walker men. Whether they would admit it or not, both of them were hurting. More than hurting: shocked and horrified at the turn of events. Travis may not have always been the most observant person, but he'd never deliberately hurt someone. Lenore had crossed that line, and Rod hated that it was because of him.

Once this shock wore off, would Travis resent Rod? Resent that choosing him meant Travis lost his mother? He shook his head. It was too much to think about. Too much to take in. He wasn't normally a fatalistic person, but only the passing of time would help them all heal *and* reveal what scars might be left behind.

"Mom said you were gay, but I didn't believe her." Rod's attention refocused from his boyfriend to his dad's step-kids. The two were close to identical, but the one who spoke was shorter. Rod thought his name was Alex.

"Why not?"

Alex shrugged. "I figured she was trying to make me feel better."

"Feel better about?" There was no way Rod was putting words in that boy's mouth.

He shrugged again. "About being gay too."

Morgan came up to stand protectively next to his brother, a stubborn expression on his face. Rod appreciated him having his brother's back. He noticed that both his dad and Meg had made themselves scarce. The back door was ajar; they must have gone to check out the garden.

"Are you thirsty? I think Travis bought some of that fancy fizzy water. Sorry, no soda."

Each of the boys grudgingly accepted a can of pricey water. Rod could not figure out why Travis bought it, but he had to admit he liked the cran-raspberry flavored one.

He popped open a can for himself and leaned back against the counter.

"Did you come out recently?"

Alex took a swig of water before he answered. Morgan watched, still protective.

"I guess. It wasn't on purpose, though." He looked down at the kitchen floor.

When it became clear he wasn't going to say any more, Morgan chipped in. "One of the jock assholes, who is probably gay too, told the whole school that Alex had tried to kiss him."

"I did try to kiss him. He's the one who kept 'accidentally' running into me on my way home from school. He tried to kiss me first. I don't know why he did that. I wasn't going to say anything."

Rod sighed. God, why were humans so fucking stupid? "He's probably afraid."

"That's what Mom said, but he doesn't have the whole school calling him a faggot, does he? No, he made sure it was me."

"Has it been bad?"

Alex rolled his eyes. "Duh. The teachers think they have it all under control and shit, but when they're not around it's back to calling me names and other stuff. Mom's been picking me up from school every day."

"Jesus."

"And Morgan's about to get suspended or expelled for fighting. I bet Mom sure is glad she has a fag for a son." His voice was scary and bitter. Alex had been walking a fine line of self-hatred for a while.

"I'm only gonna get suspended if those assholes don't quit bullying you."

"Are you two twins?" Rod wasn't trying to change the subject, but he couldn't tell how old the two boys were. He tried to remember if his dad had ever said.

"Nah, but we're less than a year apart." That was Morgan. "I'm the smart one, so I skipped a grade. People always think we're twins. It's fun to mess with people's heads." Alex punched his brother in the arm, hard.

Meg and his dad had their hands full.

Rod circled back to Alex's comment about his mom being upset because Alex being gay caused her trouble. "Somehow I don't think Meg is upset you're gay. I've only just gotten to meet her, but one of the very first things she made clear to me is that my being gay was not a problem. I'm pretty sure I am way less important to her than you are. It'll get better, I swear, and not every guy is an asshole like this guy in your class."

"Did you ever get bullied?"

"No, but I wasn't honest, either. Not really. I didn't come out until college. In high school I had Travis around, so even if other kids suspected I was gay, Travis would have been the one doing the pounding."

The brothers snickered, and Rod realized what he'd just said. His cheeks heated in embarrassment. "It's official. You two are a menace."

"So do we call you big brother now?"

"I prefer Rod."

Meg and Will returned from their excessively long exploration of the backyard.

"Who's hungry?" Meg asked.

They all were. The brothers sounded like they hadn't eaten in days.

THEY ENDED up at the Waterline. Rod shouldn't have been surprised; it was the premier tourist dining experience in Skagit. He hadn't been there before, mostly because when he and Travis were done with fire season they weren't fit for family dining. And of course Travis had been on a mission to get laid as much as possible, but Rod didn't want to think about that.

The table was piled high with warm bread, steamed clams, and huge onion rings (fittingly, made from Walla Walla sweet onions) when Rod's phone rang. He checked the number before answering. It wasn't Travis.

"Rod? This is Maureen James."

"Hi, Maureen. What's up?" He knew it was something about Jasper; that would be the only reason she would call.

"Well, Jasper and I were wondering if you would come by for a visit. He's had a hard few days, and it would mean a lot to him."

Rod covered the mic. "Hey guys, a friend of mine is feeling down and wants to know if I can visit. Would you mind?"

They didn't, and Rod promised Maureen they would be there within the hour. In the meantime he told his family all about Jasper.

"As far as I know, the police haven't arrested anyone yet."

"That poor boy," Meg and Will said at the same time. The brothers rolled their eyes in unison, which Rod thought was a pretty neat trick, but they also were willing to make a detour to Maureen James's house.

She actually didn't live far from Rod and Travis. Once the brothers declared they couldn't eat another bite and Will picked up the bill—Rod figured it had to cost the GNP of a small country to feed those kids—they piled in the silver minivan with Will driving.

"What kind of car do you have?" Morgan asked.

"A truck, but it was totaled in the accident, and since I couldn't drive until recently, I haven't replaced it yet."

"That sucks about your truck."

"Better the truck than him," said Will. "Where am I headed?"

JASPER WAS WAITING for them on the front porch when they arrived. He looked so much better than he had when Rod had found him at the mall, but he still looked sad. Before Rod got all the way out of the van, Jasper was plastered to him. Maureen watched from the porch.

"Hey, Jasper." Rod knelt awkwardly so he was at Jasper's level. "What's going on?"

"Nobody wants me."

"What do you mean? Let's go up to the house, okay? We can talk better there. Jasper, these folks are my dad, Will; his wife, Meg; and her sons, Alex and Morgan."

Jasper looked at the group with Rod. "Why are they here?"

"Well, they are visiting from out of town, but Maureen said it was important, so we all came to see you."

He stood slowly and offered Jasper his hand. For a second it seemed as if Jasper wouldn't take it. When he did, his grasp was almost painfully tight. Rod guessed he had been having a lot of trouble lately.

"Rod," his dad called out, "we're going to take a walk around the neighborhood. We'll be back in a little while."

"Have fun." Rod appreciated the effort his dad made to give Jasper privacy. Even nine-year-old boys needed it.

Together they went and sat on Maureen's porch. She had a porch swing that was perfect for sitting and thinking. Maureen came outside to sit with them, and Xena joined too, hopping up and squeezing in next to Jasper.

"Where's Kon?" It was rare for Kon to part from his dog, Rod had learned.

"He's at the Campbells' overseeing something to do with the newest litter of puppies."

Rod set the swing moving just slightly, enough to give a body a little distraction.

"The state has interceded and is now Jasper's guardian," Maureen said. "We found out this morning."

Rod knew from tidbits Jasper had let drop that there'd been hope of a grandparent, but it seemed now that was snuffed out.

Nothing like crushed hope to make a person feel lower than they ever had before.

"It's not fair. I'll be a good boy. Why don't they want me?"

Jasper was going to make him cry. No child should feel so alone and helpless. Xena scooted closer, laying her head on Jasper's lap. He stroked it, probably without realizing what he was doing.

"Tell me about your family. Why are they here?"

Maureen stood and went inside. Rod kept the swing moving, thinking about his answer. "Well, funny, but I haven't seen my dad in a long time. Almost since before you were a super-little kid."

"Did you make your dad mad?"

"No. But we didn't know each other very well."

"And now you do?"

"We're getting to know each other."

"Like you and me," Jasper stated.

"Just like us."

"Do they know about Phabian Frog and Todd Toad?" Jasper asked with great suspicion.

Rod laughed. "No, that's a special thing just between you and me these days."

Rod didn't think he would be going back to bus driving. Or maybe he would, but he was going to need to do something else; a part-time job wasn't going to pay the bills. His firefighting days were likely over. Fighting fires with a piece of metal in his leg did not sound like a great idea. Plus he was still recovering the strength and muscle mass he'd lost after the accident.

They sat and talked until Rod's dad and his family returned from their walk around the neighborhood. Alex and Morgan waited by the car while Will and Meg came to say hello.

"Hi Rod, I'm Meg. You must be Jasper." Jasper nodded. Rod

thought he might not say anything—Maureen said he was having trouble with strangers—but Jasper surprised him.

"Yes, are those your kids?" Jasper was looking past Meg and Will to where Alex and Morgan were waiting. Meg followed his gaze.

"Yes, Alex and Morgan. Would you like to meet them?"

Jasper leaned hard into Rod, who automatically put his arm around Jasper's shoulders.

The boys were leaning against the minivan trying to look cool and failing in a way only teenage boys can.

"They look tough, but I think they are actually pretty nice," Rod said.

"Not today." But Jasper watched them shoving each other playfully and laughing with hungry eyes, taking in everything.

ON THE WAY HOME, Meg turned around in the passenger seat, focusing her attention on Rod. "I know this is probably out of line, but I've never been one for rules anyway—"

"Meg," Will said as he drove, his tone half warning, half hoping to stop whatever she was going to say.

She ignored him. "Have you and Travis considered fostering or adoption? That little boy is clearly very attached to you, and you to him."

Alex, who was sitting between Rod and Morgan, spoke up. "Yeah, you should."

Rod glanced in the rearview mirror and caught his dad watching the exchange, a quiet smile on his face. He gave a small nod, and Rod had to look out the side window and pretend the passing scenery was really interesting. Fostering or even adopting Jasper had been on his mind, but he wasn't sure how Travis would feel about it, and it seemed really soon for them to be thinking about bringing a child—a nearly nine-year-old trau-matized boy—into their house.

He turned back. Meg was still waiting for a reply. "It seems soon, I guess."

Meg nodded and turned back around. "That's true; there can be times that aren't the best for whatever reason, but I don't think you always can pick when the 'right' time is. Think about it, and maybe make a few phone calls. I imagine the process is reasonably streamlined, and we all know how many kids in foster care need placement."

Rod looked out the window again. Meg's words were too much and not enough. Every time he had lunch or dinner with Jasper or took him to the park around the corner from Maureen's, he thought about adoption. It was hard for him to leave, and while Jasper didn't cry, Rod knew it was hard for him too. Maureen was a great foster parent, and she seemed to specialize in difficult cases, but Jasper needed a permanent home.

"We think you would be good at it. Jasper seemed pretty cool, even if he is nine." That was Morgan.

"You didn't actually meet him." Rod looked over at his step-brother. Morgan shrugged the timeless shrug of a teenager.

The rest of the short trip back to the house was quiet. As they all got out of the car, Will caught his elbow, holding him back for a minute. Meg and the boys headed to the porch.

"For what it's worth, I support you no matter what you decide. I agree with Meg and the boys, though. Jasper, or any child, would thrive in your care."

"Thanks, Dad."


ROD'S DAD and family stayed in Skagit for a few more days. The activity wore Rod out more than he was willing to admit. Each day he slumped into bed exhausted from entertaining and exploring what seemed like most of western Washington. Travis was a trouper, and even Michael joined them for dinner the last evening. He was still in town dealing with the police and lawyers. Lenore didn't want anything to do with any of them, not even her husband of nearly thirty years.

Every spare minute, between all the other things going on, he thought about Jasper, about fostering, about how to bring the subject up with Travis. In his heart of hearts Rod knew Travis would be onboard, but kids—their own or an adopted or fostered kid—would be a huge change, and they had barely been together as a couple for a few months.

He reminded himself he'd known Travis for almost twenty years. Travis was a generous, caring person who went out of his way to help others. Wasn't that how they'd become friends in the first place?

The Monday after his dad left, Rod made a few phone calls. Just to see. Hours later he was still on his phone and laptop (at the same time), asking and answering questions and filling out forms.

Just in case. Just in case Travis agreed.

Tuesday he talked to Gloria about fostering or adopting Jasper. Now that the state was Jasper's legal guardian, Rod felt like the time to act was sooner rather than later. He had waking and sleeping nightmares about Jasper being placed in a faceless, soulless home where he was mistreated and neglected. Where there would be no stories.

"Sweetie, you need to quit second-guessing yourself. Your Travis is a man made for family. You need to quit overthinking things."

Ha, Rod thought, he had a gold medal in overthinking. He was practically an Olympic champion.

"It seems to me that Travis is nothing if not honest. If he

thinks the timing is wrong or—and I have a hard time imagining this—he doesn't want children, he will tell you. And then you can talk about it."

"It's hard to argue against that logic."

"Of course it is," Gloria replied.

Rod planned on bringing the subject up with Travis that evening, but he and Michael were busy dealing with the legal ramifications of what Lenore had done. The last thing Rod wanted to do was add to Travis's stress, and since Michael was heading back east of the Cascades the next morning, he figured it could wait.

Wednesday morning he was going to talk to Travis, but one thing led to another, and the next thing he knew they were both hot and sweaty and Rod couldn't form words, much less a compelling argument as to why they should open their household to a traumatized kid.

Travis pressed him into the mattress with his body weight and kissed him again, running his tongue along the line of Rod's jaw one more time before sucking on his lower lip. Rod had already come, but he still felt a spark of desire along his spine. If they had time, he would definitely be up for more.

"I gotta take a shower," he grumbled.

"We could take a shower together." Travis waggled his eyebrows.

"I do actually have to be at the doctor's in," he looked at the digital clock on his side of the bed, "shit, an hour, and I don't think a shower with you will fit in that time span."

Travis stuck his lower lip out, but his clear blue eyes were smiling. "Fine. You go first."

He still barely made it to his appointment on time.

## 20

Travis had to blink away tears, the small sheet of paper he held in his hand going blurry.

You asked me to be the best man at your wedding, and I said I would. I will.

There's something I should have told you much earlier. Obviously now it doesn't matter... but you are more to me than my best friend. I know now, for certain, that you don't feel the same way.

I get it, I do.

But I'm going to need time to sort myself out. I hope you understand.

Sorry to leave without saying goodbye.

Your best man, always,

Rod

There was a throat-clearing sound. Travis looked up from the note. The clerk behind the counter pushed his glasses up his nose and raised his dark eyebrows, waiting for Travis to decide if the price he was offering for the game was right.

Travis was at loose ends. His dad had left for home again, and Rod was at his final doctor's appointment and then his standing lunch date with Gloria and Jasper. Trav had decided to finally put up the gaming system in the living room. With everything going on and the fact that once Travis and Rod went to bed at night neither one of them was thinking about playing video games, those last few boxes had been shoved against the living room wall and abandoned. As he'd stared at the games, he'd realized a fact about living with Rod: they didn't need two of everything.

So he'd done a little research and found a place that bought used games. Instead of unpacking anything, he'd just taken the whole box of his games. The clerk had been going through each one checking for scratches and that the title matched the box. When he'd opened the one now in Travis's hand, both of them had been surprised to see a piece of notebook paper folded inside the case.

A note from Rod seven months ago was not what he'd been expecting when he unfolded it.

The words were hastily written, and there was something at the end that Rod had scribbled out.

"Hey, you want to sell these or what?"

"Uh, yeah. Thanks."

Travis exited the shop feeling oddly light-headed. He couldn't believe he hadn't found the note months ago. The June sunlight seemed brighter than it had when he went into the store. He laughed. It probably *was* brighter, as it was around noon, but it felt brighter to his soul.

The shop was located in a part of town that mixed residential, retail, and semi-industrial. A holdover from when Skagit zoning was a little wacky. Many small businesses had opened up in what were originally single-family homes.

Next to the DiscMan (Travis thought the name was very clever) was a shop called Otto's Erotica. Travis was debating going in and browsing for something a little kinky—he loved it when Rod blushed—when the front door burst open and someone took the stairs at a leap. He—it was a he, that's about all Travis saw—landed on the sidewalk, glanced at Travis, and raced off in the other direction.

The door to the sex shop swung shut with a bang. And then there was silence. Travis didn't hesitate; he ran up the steps and inside.

"Hello? Anyone here?" At first he thought there was no answer; then he heard a faint groan. Behind the front counter a man was half lying, half sitting on the floor. The cash drawer was open but looked empty.

"Have you been robbed? Are you okay?" Travis asked as he came around the counter. The man peered at him from under a tangle of dark hair.

"Are you here to rescue me?"

There was a lump forming on his forehead, and his cheek was scraped.

"Did that guy hit you?"

"Who are you?" The other man struggled to his feet. The top of his head came up to about Travis's shoulder.

"Travis Walker, you?"

"I'm Otto, I own this place. And no, he didn't hit me. He pushed me down, and I hit my head on the counter. He did take all the cash I had, though. Too bad for him that most people don't carry cash these da— Hey, what are you doing?"

The 911 operator took the information from Travis, and after she made sure that Otto wasn't in danger anymore, she said an officer would be over as soon as possible.

"Just my luck, a good Samaritan. Can't a bad Samaritan find me one of these days? Do you know how much paperwork this is going to be? They're never going to catch the guy."

"What about cameras?" Travis pointed to one in the corner over the cash register.

Otto looked to where Travis was pointing. "Oh, ha, no. That's a cleverly disguised shoebox. Do you see any cords?"

Now that he was looking closer, he could see it was just a white-painted box with a tube, only vaguely looking like a surveillance camera. "Well, that sucks."

"So, what brings you to the neighborhood? Just out and about do-gooding, were you?" Otto seemed determined to keep the conversation light, so Travis obliged him, but he wasn't leaving until the cops arrived. He could see Otto trembling.

Travis didn't know what to do with himself and didn't want to intimidate Otto with his size, so he stayed on the other side of the counter, leaning his hip against it.

"I was over at DiscMan selling a bunch of games." Somehow Travis ended up telling Otto the whole story of how he and Rod finally got together.

Otto's dark eyes widened. "And you just found the note today? While you were next door? That is so romantic! It makes getting robbed completely worth it. I need to hear everything again. Repeat, with more detail."

A few customers tried to come in, but Travis waved them off, saying the store was closed for inventory and to try again tomorrow. By the time the two of them heard the crunch of gravel outside announcing the arrival of the SkPD, Travis had been through the story twice.

"Your own mom. Tragic," Otto breathed. "What's going to happen?"

"She was released, and my ex didn't press charges. I guess since she doesn't have a criminal record, nothing much will happen. I feel terrible for my dad; he had no idea. He tried to talk to her, and I know he's paying legal fees and she has to go to counseling, but she didn't even go home. She's staying with a church friend instead. I guess they are separated."

Otto shook his head. "Your dad sounds amazing. It's good to

know there are people like him in the world and they aren't all going to turn on us."

There was a tap, and the front door pushed open. Travis was startled to see the same hulking blond detective who had responded when Rod found Jasper. But Skagit wasn't all that big, he supposed.

Otto stopped talking. Travis wasn't people smart, but it was pretty clear that Otto was a talker, and being quiet meant he was nervous again. Travis stood and met the detective at the threshold.

"Travis Walker." He held out a hand. "Good—or I guess not good—to see you again. Otto's over here." He led the detective over to the counter where Otto was waiting. Otto had backed up against the wall with his arms wrapped protectively around himself.

Jorgensen took his suit jacket off as he approached.

"Here, wrap this around your shoulders. You look like you might be going into shock."

Mutely, Otto took the proffered jacket and wrapped it around himself. He was enough smaller than the detective that the jacket was more like a robe.

"Is there somewhere else we can go so I can take your statement? Maybe we should have someone check out that bump on your head."

Otto declined the suggestion of medical attention. "I live upstairs," he replied with a shrug.

"Is it okay if we go up? I think you'll be more comfortable in a different space. Am I right?"

Otto nodded.

"Do you want me to come along?" Travis asked.

"Might as well get your statement while I'm at it." Detective Jorgensen seemed resigned to Travis's presence.

"I wasn't asking you, I was asking Otto."

"I know."

Otto seemed surprised Travis had asked permission, but after a second he nodded. After shutting and locking the front door, he led them toward the back of the store where a colorful curtain hung. He pulled it aside to reveal a doorway and a set of stairs heading upward. They followed him upstairs, Otto keeping the detective's jacket tightly wrapped around himself.

The apartment took up the second floor of the house; even so, it wasn't very large. At the top of the stairs, what used to be two bedrooms had been combined to create a living room and tiny kitchen. There was a deck the size of the porch roof that looked out over the street. There was a small bathroom and a bedroom, and that was it.

It was probably perfect for Otto, but with Travis and Detective Jorgensen, the space felt very small. It didn't take too long to get Otto's and Travis's statements. Travis had texted Rod that he was going to be late picking him up; hopefully Gloria and Jasper wouldn't drag him into mischief before Travis could get there.

Jorgensen stood up from the chair he'd been occupying. Otto stood too, and again Travis was struck by the sheer bulk of the detective.

"How are you not a cowboy or something?" The words came from Otto, but Travis had been thinking them.

The detective smiled. Travis had to admit that the man was incredibly handsome, especially when he broke out a smile. "If I was a cowboy, who would catch all the bad guys?"

Travis watched as a breaker in Otto's brain short-circuited. He shook his head and muttered something, but all Travis caught was "horses," "Levi's," and "criminal." Otto realized both men were watching him and turned a shade of red Travis hadn't thought possible.

"Whatever, fine, no cowboys. This day hasn't been all that bad. Even though I was robbed, and the coward took the fifty dollars I had in the cash box, it brought two of the best-looking men I've seen in far, far, too long into the store. I'm calling that a win. And I got to hear the best story." He turned to Travis. "I need to know the end of this, okay? You can't just waltz in here, save me from a robber, tell me a love story, and then not come back and tell me the ending."

"I didn't save you from a robber."

"Whatever, details. Promise."

"I will come back and bring Rod with me so he can meet you. I promise."

Jorgensen followed Travis back downstairs and outside. Otto let them out and locked up behind them. He left the "Closed" sign up, saying he'd had enough for one day, and promised Jorgensen he would have a security company come out and install real cameras.

Jorgensen's ugly, obviously police issue, sedan was parked next to Travis's truck.

"The kid's case is still open, but there's not a lot of leads."

Jorgensen did remember him. Travis hadn't been sure; the detective had been almost entirely focused on Otto.

"Rod's been staying updated, as much as he can through Maureen James."

"It sucks. From everything we know, Belinda Ransom was a single mom trying to make it. There's no sign of Jasper's father, if she even told anyone who he was. That's about all we've got."

Travis thought about the little boy Rod was having lunch with and about family and what family meant. He felt lucky to have his dad and his sister (and Rod) at his back. So many people had lost more than he had, and it was pure luck. He could have been born into any family. He was lucky to have been born into the one he had.

Yes, he was still trying to get his head around his mother's behavior, and he probably would never be able to understand her reasons, but all in all they were healthier now without her hate seeping into everything they did.

Family was Abs and his dad, of course, but also Rod, as well as Gloria, Rod's dad, and his family. Cameron and Ira, probably. And Jasper Ransom... Travis suspected he would fit well into the motley crew that made up his reimagined family.

# 21

———

"What?" Rod stared at Travis, but Travis was watching the road.

"I witnessed a robbery today, and I promised to take you to meet Otto, the owner of the store, because he thinks our story is romantic."

Rod slumped back against the seat, crossing his arms over his chest. "What's romantic about me being stupid?"

"I found the note."

"What note?" Rod had no idea what Travis was talking about.

Now Travis did quickly glance at Rod. "The note you left me at Thanksgiving."

Warmth crept into his face. Rod knew he was blushing. "Well, that's embarrassing. I thought you found it months ago."

"Why is it embarrassing?" Travis seemed genuinely confused.

"Jeez, Trav, I was too much of a coward to tell you how I felt, so I wrote a note and ran away. That is embarrassing."

"You didn't know, it's not as if I gave any clues. You shouldn't feel that way. I didn't even *know* I loved you. How stupid is that?"

"Yeah, but I do anyway." They were driving up one of Skagit's busier streets where lots of shops and restaurants were located. The truck was reflected in the windows as they passed by.

Neither spoke for a little while. Travis was probably mulling over Rod's behavior. Then, of course, they both spoke at once.

"Trav—"

"What do—"

Rod chuckled. He was nervous as hell. "You go."

"No, I was just talking. What were you going to say?"

He took a breath. He could do this, right? He and Travis were solid; if they disagreed, it wouldn't be the end of their relationship. They could talk things through like big kids.

"I've been thinking." Rod couldn't decide if he was going to stare out the windshield or at Travis to watch his reaction. He decided on Travis. "Um, have you ever thought about kids? Like having them? I mean, not *having them* having them, because except in fiction that is just not possible, but have you ever thought about maybe adoption or something? Or fostering?"

Travis grinned, the big one that Rod loved, that looked like he'd just won the lottery. "Are we talking about kids in general or *a* kid specifically? Because yes."

"What yes? I mean, yes, I am, you bastard, you know I am talking about Jasper." He punched him in the shoulder. "Sometimes I hate you. Would you consider fostering Jasper?"

Travis rubbed his biceps, but he was still grinning. "That hurt!"

"It was supposed to."

They turned the corner to their street. Before answering, Travis pulled his truck to the curb and set it in park. "Do we have to get a minivan? I am not driving one of those."

"Trav, I was thinking about one specific kid, not a human zoo. No, but I do need to replace my truck. How did we get off track? Wait, are you saying yes?"

"As long as we have a lock on our bedroom door." Trav unbuckled his seat belt and leaned into Rod. His hand came up and caressed Rod's cheek, then he kissed him. They made out in the truck for a few minutes like a couple of teenagers. "But seriously, you shouldn't ever be embarrassed to tell me, or ask me, stuff. I already know everything about you. Remember seventh grade?"

Rod huffed a little laugh. It was true, Trav did know everything. "I can't explain why I feel shy or nervous sometimes. There's a part of me that's always scared, I guess. A part that has a really hard time believing that we are for real. That part of me is always second-guessing and reminding me of the times I've failed. I know it's stupid, and I try not to listen, but when I am feeling uncertain, that voice can be hard to ignore."

"Yes. Yes. Yes."

"Yes what?" Rod had lost the thread of the conversation between sucking on Travis's face and exposing a part of himself he was ashamed of.

"Yes, I love you. Yes, it's forever. Yes, I want to see if we can make Jasper a part of our family." He leaned away and opened his door, stepping out onto the street.

Rod sat for a minute, blinking, wondering if he had heard right and knowing that he had. He unlocked his door and nearly strangled himself trying to get out.

"You need to unbuckle, dude. Now, *that* is something to be embarrassed about."

"Fuck off."

"No."

Travis grabbed him in a familiar headlock-slash-hug. When he was released, Rod found himself on the receiving end of another passionate kiss. When he was done, Travis grabbed Rod's hand, lacing their fingers together as they walked to the front door.

"So, what do we need to do?" Travis asked.

## 22

"Dad," Travis started, "I know this is a bad time, but you're here, and I want to talk to you about something. Something I've already mentioned, but now I think I'm really ready."

Michael glanced at him before focusing his attention back on the road. They were on their way to the farmers market to meet up with Brandon Campbell and his wife, Stephanie. "Shoot."

Lenore had served his dad with divorce papers the week before, citing irreconcilable differences. Michael had signed them, telling Abby and Travis there was no point in fighting it. Now came the hard part: splitting up two lives that had been, by and large, lived together. Travis felt terrible for what his dad must be going through.

When his dad had told him, Travis had automatically offered an invitation. "Come visit for a few days."

Michael was leaving the lawyers to do the hard work of sorting out finances, for now. Most of the family land was held by the business, something Travis's mom had never had much of a hand in. Regardless, it was going to be a long road for both of them.

Travis had tried reaching out to Lenore after the incident, but after months of horrible texts, all he had now was silence. She refused to talk to him in any way. It was surreal. He didn't understand how his mother, or anyone's parent, could turn on or off affection like it was a commodity.

Something he recognized as loss hovered along the edge of his consciousness, but Travis pushed it away. Whatever corner his mother had turned in the past months or maybe even years, it affected his dad much worse than himself. Now he understood what Abigail had been talking about, and he'd been blind to it.

"Quit thinking so hard over there, and tell me what's on your mind."

"I've been thinking about grapes, Dad."

"Grapes? Yeah, you mean wine?" His dad glanced at him again.

Travis nodded. "You know that parcel that grandpa left me, I want to put grapes on it—cabernet or Syrah maybe—and see how that goes. I want to open a tasting room out here. I mean, we could do one there too, but I want to open one here in Skagit. Until the grapes are mature, I can buy them from other producers in the state. I think with the farmers market and the demand for local produce—as long as it's well planned, I could do well here." The words came out in a rush, but Travis had done a lot of preliminary research and knew this was something he could do.

"What do you need from me?"

The question caught him off guard. "I don't expect anything. But I want to make sure, I guess, that it's okay with you."

"I'd like to be a part, not as Walker Enterprises but as your dad. Would that be okay?"

Tears caught him off guard too. The road ahead blurred. He

was a mess these days. He tried to wipe his eyes without his dad noticing.

"Yeah, Dad, I think that would be okay, more than okay. I want to show you something."

"I thought we were meeting some friends of yours."

"We are, they'll still be there when we get there. Turn left at the next intersection."

WHEN THEY FINALLY ARRIVED AT the farmers market and made their way to Brandon Campbell's stall, his dad had called the realtor and his lawyers. And Abigail. As they strode down the crowded walkway, his dad kept tossing out ideas for a winery and tasting room. It had been a long time—if ever—since Travis had seen his dad that excited about something. Maybe they were both starting over, and maybe that wasn't as frightening when you had family at your back.

Brandon's stall was smack in the middle of the market. As a founding member and business member who made regular large donations, he was given the optimal location. Funny thing, Travis thought no matter where the stall was located his produce would always sell out. Brandon and Stephanie were well respected, Travis had learned, not only for their organic produce but for the not-so-secret work Brandon did with homeless youth in the area.

As Travis and his dad approached, Brandon spotted them and came out from behind the colorful display.

"Brandon, this is my dad, Michael Walker."

The two men shook hands, and Brandon's enormous shaggy dog lumbered over to see what the fuss was about.

"This is Pronto," Brandon said by way of introduction.

"Pronto?" His dad repeated automatically, giving the dog a scratch on the head.

"He's not, but Stephanie and I like to give our dogs a challenge."

It didn't take Travis long to fill Brandon in on his idea for a tasting room and boutique winery.

"There's a lot of hops grown here too, and they don't take so long to mature— from what I understand, there is a waiting list these days. Fresh Washington hops are very popular."

Travis was so full of ideas, and hope, and the beginnings of a plan that he couldn't keep his emotions in check. He grabbed his dad and squeezed him as tightly as he could, lifting him about an inch off the ground before putting him back down.

His dad pretended to brush himself off and straighten his clothing, but he was smiling broadly, something Travis hadn't seen a whole lot of recently. It was great to see it.

A woman at the fresh-cut flower stall next door called over, "What's all the excitement about?"

"Life is good!" Travis yelled back.

"Trix, come meet some new friends of mine." Brandon motioned for her to come over. Trix whipped out a handwritten sign that said, "All bouquets $10, please pay into the retirement bucket," placing it next to a can she had just for that purpose.

Soon enough there was an impromptu party going on at Brandon's stall. Brandon was introducing them to people right and left. There was no way Travis was going to remember all the names, but he had a thick stack of business cards in his back pocket.

## 23

"Why are you making me get up?" Travis had dragged Rod out of bed on a Saturday morning, insisting he had a surprise for him. The only surprise Rod was interested in was an early-morning blowjob, but that didn't seem to be in the cards.

"Get dressed. I want to show you something."

"Is there coffee involved? If I can't have a blow job, I want coffee."

Travis laughed. God, Rod loved his laugh.

"If I promise coffee now *and* a blow job later, will you quit bitching and come with me?"

"Fine." Rod pouted.

"You're going the wrong way for coffee."

"I thought," Travis replied patiently, "that we would stop at the new place, The Last Drop. It's on our way."

"I would have known that if you would tell me where we're going."

Travis pulled to a stop in front of a house that had been

converted into a cute café. There was a line of people out the door, and Rod winced.

"That's for sit-down, don't worry."

Rod turned his head with a snarky reply to find Travis had leaned across the armrest. He planted a quick, hot kiss full of promise on Rod's lips, and all grouchy thoughts fled. Rod flicked out his tongue to taste Travis, loving that he was allowed, that Travis was his.

"None of that. I'm not putting on a show." Travis leaned back and clicked open his seat belt. "Come on."

The Last Drop was epically cool. The owner had gutted the interior of the house, making it one big space. In the center was a horseshoe-shaped bar with a glittering espresso machine where beer taps would usually be. One side of the bar was clearly the to-go area, and the other had mismatched tables and chairs for seating. A doorway led out to a porch that wrapped two-thirds of the way around the house. There were tables outside as well. Every seat was full.

"This place is incredible."

"It's amazing, isn't it? They've only been open a month."

Travis didn't let Rod linger. Soon they were back out on the road, but not for long. This time when Travis stopped his truck, they were parked in front of a run-down property not far from town. At one point it had been pretty isolated, but Skagit had grown. The house looked to be unlivable from where Rod sat, safely in the truck. The barn was pretty, though.

"Okay, I'll bite. Why are we parked here?"

"Come on." Travis got out and began to make his way toward the barn.

Rod, as he always did, followed. "Travis, isn't this private property?"

Travis ignored him and kept walking toward the barn, unashamedly opening the gate and sauntering through. He rolled aside the barn door like he owned it and disappeared inside.

Inside, the barn was filled with dappled light that found its in way through the hay drop as well as gaps between the siding and roof beams. Travis stopped in the center and turned in a slow circle before his gaze focused on Rod. "What do you think?"

"It's beautiful," he answered truthfully, "just beautiful."

"I have a plan." Travis waggled his eyebrows.

"How many times in our lives have you started a sentence with that exact phrase?"

"Mmmm, come here."

Rod was never going to be able to resist Travis. He didn't want to, and he didn't have to. He went. Travis wrapped his strong arms around Rod before whispering in his ear.

"This is the future home of the Walker Winery tasting room. See that pink piece of paper over there?"

Rod couldn't see from the angle he was at. Travis turned him 180 degrees, keeping his arms wrapped around him as if he was afraid Rod might run away. There was a small piece of paper tacked to an interior wall. It fluttered slightly as a breeze snuck in.

"That piece of paper is the beginning of everything."

"Is this what you've been secretly working on?"

"Yeah. I didn't want to say anything until I knew all the wrinkles were ironed out. Or at least that this would eventually happen."

"What, exactly, is happening?"

"Do you want it in order, or do you want a good news–bad news kind of scenario? Or..." Travis broke off his meandering when Rod tried to turn and pinch him. Or maybe tickle him. Or throw him down in the vestiges of hay and fuck him silly.

Something in his expression must've told Travis what Rod

was thinking. Travis ground against him, chuckling evilly. "While I have every intention of making use of the barn, Michael is on his way. I don't think that's the kind of exhibitionism you are into."

"Damn." Rod thought bad thoughts, trying to will his semi away.

Travis rested his chin on Rod's shoulder. "You know how my grandpa left me that smallish parcel? Dad and I are going to plant it with grapes. In the meantime, while my grapes mature, I'm going to buy grapes and start making wine. This will be the tasting room, and there will be a cold room and a chiller. We'll have to build for that, but the barn is where we'll start."

"We?"

"Do you want to be Beton-Walker or Walker-Beton? Personally I think Walker-Beton has a better ring to it. Kind of like this ring here." Travis pulled a small fabric bag out of his pocket and held it out in the palm of his hand.

Rod stared at the bag, then stared at Travis. Then stared again at the bag before reaching out with a shaking hand to take it. His fingers were too thick and clumsy all of a sudden, and everything was watery.

"I can't open it," Rod whispered. The barn was quiet around them, a comfort.

Travis opened the bag and shook out a gold band into his palm.

"I had to guess your size." He cleared his throat before shuffling around to get down on one knee. "Rod Beton, you've had my back since I was nine. You've been with me through thick and thin. Will you spend the rest of your life with me? Will you marry me?"

Rod looked at his best friend, blurry because tears were leaking from his eyes. "Yes, Travis, I will marry you." His voice was small in the quiet, but loud to his heart.

He pulled Travis off his knees and kissed him until there was no more oxygen and he had to come up for air. Travis used his thumb to wipe the moisture from Rod's cheek. "Why are you crying?"

Rod wasn't sure he would be able to put what he was feeling into words, but he sure as hell would try.

"Travis, I've had this secret dream for so long. I never believed it would come true, that you would want me back in the same way. That you would want to marry me. I feel overwhelmed... and scared you are going to change your mind."

"Rod," Travis took Rod's face between his hands, "I know everything about you. I love you. I've always loved you, even when I didn't know what the word meant. I'm not changing my mind."

The lump in his throat was difficult for Rod to speak around. "I love you too."

"I know. I know."

This kiss was gentle and filled with promise, not just of that night but of tomorrow and as many tomorrows as they could fit in their lives together. Travis tightened his grip on Rod's waist, making sure there was no room between them as he swept his tongue into Rod's mouth. Their tongues met in a dance as old as time itself. Rod didn't want to stop. "We've got to stop or, uh."

Travis was breathing heavily. "Yeah. Wouldn't want my dad to find us. But I don't ever want you thinking anyone else is my best man. Come on, let's go meet him at the truck."

# EPILOGUE

The black-and-white fluff ball was nearly as large as Jasper, but he insisted on holding the leash even though the puppy was going to pull him over any moment. Brandon had provided them with a special leash and collar with the puppy's name, Crusher, embroidered on them. Rod wasn't entirely sure how (or when) they'd agreed to a puppy, but once they'd known for certain that Jasper was coming to them, somehow there was a puppy included. Travis's friend Brandon wouldn't let them pay him, either, claiming the puppy was the runt of the litter and needed a special home to live in. Rod was pretty sure they'd been played, but watching Jasper with the dog, he knew they'd made the right decision.

Bringing Jasper home hadn't been an easy process. There had been an astounding number of hoops to jump through. Rod understood the state had to be careful, but when Jasper cried, it was difficult to explain they needed to wait and do everything in the right order. Even now there were still last t's and i's to be crossed and dotted. But they were closer to being a family.

Gloria Browning had played a huge part. She gave character

references for both of them, and her standing in the community meant a lot to the officials in the Department of Health and Human Services.

They'd been able to jump the gun a little because Maureen had a pair of siblings come to her who needed her undivided attention, so the case worker had authorized the move from her house to Travis and Rod's.

Last night they'd stayed up past two a.m. painting and putting the finishing touches on Jasper's bedroom and making sure they had all the supplies for Crusher. Rod couldn't believe they were bringing home a puppy and Jasper on the same day. He was excited. He was nervous. He was ready.

They were taking the long way back to their place because Maureen and Kon were racing over to be a part of the surprise family barbeque they'd planned for Jasper. Will, Meg, and the boys—who'd recently announced they were moving to Skagit—would be there, as would Michael, the Campbells, and a few other friends. Rod had managed to contact Shanda, Sydney's mom, and she was bringing Maurice as well. He hoped it wasn't too much, but he wanted Jasper to know how happy he and Travis were that he would be living with them. When the adoption was official, they would have an even bigger party.

"Rod?" Jasper asked.

"Yeah?" He glanced in the rearview mirror. Jasper was literally being crushed by Crusher.

"Do you think my mom is watching over me?"

"Like an angel?"

"Kinda, but there's no such thing as angels."

Rod nodded. "Yeah, I do. I think that's how come I was at the mall that day with Gloria."

Jasper looked thoughtful for a moment. Travis gripped Rod's knee, giving him a squeeze.

"I think she'd like Crusher, and Stripey."

"Me too."

That seemed to satisfy Jasper. He went back to petting Crusher.

Rod took the turn to their street. He and Travis made eye contact. Travis mouthed, "I love you."

"Is that Alex and Morgan's car?" Jasper asked.

It was. It looked like the last of their short list of guests had arrived.

"It is! Let's go say hi and introduce them to Crusher."

Jasper and the dog tumbled out of the SUV Rod had bought in lieu of a minivan. Jasper held the leash in a tight grip while the puppy tugged him over to sniff at a patch of grass.

Travis asked, "How about if I hold him for a second so you can say hi to Alex. I think he must be in the backyard."

While Will and Meg's family had been in town over the past month or so looking at schools and houses, Alex and Jasper had become unlikely friends. Or maybe not unlikely, but with the age gap, unusual at the very least. Rod thought Alex felt a little protective of Jasper.

"Okay!" Where any other kid might have dropped the leash and run, Jasper carefully handed it to Travis. "Got it?"

"Got it," Trav confirmed.

They both watched Jasper trot around the side of the house and then heard the click of the gate being opened, followed by voices calling out, "Welcome home!"

To his surprise, when they made their way into the backyard, Rod saw Jasper giving Detective Jorgensen a fierce hug. Asking the officer had been a last-minute decision, but it seemed to have been a good one. The other guests were protecting the cake Rod had ordered (Travis had tried to bake one, but the evidence of its existence had been removed to the garbage) from Xena.

Jasper let go of the big detective, coming over to Travis to retake Crusher's leash. "Rod?"

He bent down to hear what Jasper was saying. "Yeah?"

"Thanks for having a party for Crusher. He was a little worried about missing his family."

"This party is for you, Jasper."

"Yeah, I know." He scuffed a toe against the grass. "But I don't want Crusher's feelings to be hurt."

Rod smiled and hugged their foster (for now) son tightly until he squeaked, "Lemme go." Rod did, and Jasper and Crusher ran off to check out the cake and other treats sitting on the picnic table.

As he stood up, he felt a little dizzy, but Travis was right there to make sure he didn't fall.

"You okay?" Travis's warm hand was a comfort at the small of his back.

"I'm more than okay. I'm the luckiest man in the world."

Travis slid his arm around Rod's waist, whispering in Rod's ear, "I'm pretty sure we're both lucky... or going to get lucky— one of those for sure."

WHEN IT RAINS, is the next Shielded Hearts book. Get ready for a wild ride with SkPD officer Beto Hernandez and the elusive Carsten Quinn. *Who is Carsten Quinn, where does he fit in Beto's investigation? Beto tries to stay away from Carsten but their undeniable chemistry keeps him close.*

DID you begin in the middle? Storm Season is the first in the Shielded Hearts series. Get started with surly FBI agent Adam Klay and sweet Micah Ryan.

DON'T MISS another first in series, Conspiracy Theory, the first in the Veiled Intentions series. *Niall's known nothing but betrayal. All Mat wants is Niall's heart. What will it take for Mat to coax Niall in from the cold?*

# A THANK YOU FROM ELLE

If you enjoyed His Best Man, I would greatly appreciate if you would let your friends know so they can experience Rod, Travis and the rest of the gang as well. As with all of my books, I have enabled lending on all platforms in which it is allowed to make it easy to share with a friend. If you leave a review for His Best Man, or any of my books. on the site from which you purchased the book, Goodreads or your own blog, I would love to read it! Email me the link at elle@ellekeaton.com

Keep up-to-date with new releases and sales, *The Highway to Elle* hits your in-box approximately every two weeks, sometimes more sometimes less. I include deals, freebies and new releases as well as a sort of rambling running commentary on what *this* author's life is like. I'd love to have you aboard! I also have a reader group called the Highway to Elle, come say hi!

# ABOUT ELLE

Elle hails from the northwest corner of the US known for, rain, rain, and more rain. She pens Shielded Hearts, the Veiled Intentions, Home in Hollyridge and Crimes of the Heart series' all set in the Pacific Northwest. Elle is chief cook and bottle washer, the one always asking 'where are my keys and/or wallet' and 'why are there cats?' (This question not yet answered).

Elle *loves* both cats and dogs, Star Wars and Star Trek, pineapple on pizza, and is known to start crossword puzzles with ballpoint pen.

Thank you for supporting this Indie Author,

Elle

Lightning Source UK Ltd.
Milton Keynes UK
UKHW020431031121
393296UK00011B/887

9 781393 254621